PENGUIN BOOKS

MY DATELESS DIARY

R. K. Narayan was born in Madras, South India, and educated there and at Maharaja's College in Mysore. His first novel *Swami and Friends* (1935) and its successor *The Bachelor of Arts* (1937) are both set in the enchanting fictional territory of Malgudi. Other 'Malgudi' novels are *The Dark Room* (1938), *The English Teacher* (1945), *Mr. Sampath* (1949), *The Financial Expert* (1952), *The Man Eater of Malgudi* (1961), *The Vendor of Sweets* (1967), *The Painter of Signs* (1977), *A Tiger for Malgudi* (1983), and *Talkative Man* (1986). His novel *The Guide* (1958) won him the National Prize of the Indian Literary Academy, his country's highest literary honour. He was awarded in 1980 the A.C. Benson Medal by the Royal Society of Literature and in 1981 he was made an Honorary Member of the American Academy and Institute of Arts and Letters. As well as five collections of short stories, *A Horse and Two Goats, An Astrologer's Day and Other Stories, Lawley Road, Under the Banyan Tree and Malgudi Days*, he has published a travel book, *The Emerald Route*, three collections of essays, *A Writer's Nightmare, Next Sunday* and *Reluctant Guru*, three books on the Indian epics, and a volume of memoirs, *My Days*.

R. K. NARAYAN

MY DATELESS DIARY

An American Journey

PENGUIN BOOKS

Penguin Books (India) Ltd, 72-B Himalaya House
Kasturba Gandhi Marg, New Delhi–110 001. India
Penguin Books Ltd, Harmondsworth, Middlesex, England
Viking Penguin Inc., 40 West 23rd Street, New York, N.Y. 10010, U.S.A.
Penguin Books Australia Ltd, Ringwood, Victoria, Australia
Penguin Books Canada Ltd, 2801 John Street, Markham, Ontario, Canada L3R1B4
Penguin Books (N.Z.) Ltd, 182–190 Wairau Road, Auckland 10, New Zealand

First Published by Indian Thought Publications 1964
Published by Orient Paperbacks 1969

Published in Penguin Books 1988

Made and printed in India by
Ananda Offset Private Limited, Calcutta
Typeset in Times Roman

CONTENTS

FOREWORD

Datelessness has its limit. Sooner or later the seal of date shows up even in the most indifferently maintained diary. For example, the portion describing the progress of my novel, *The Guide,* is a date-seal, if you are watchful. The following pages arose out of a day-to-day journal kept when I first visited the United States of America on an invitation by the Rockefeller Foundation. Arriving in New York, I crossed to the west coast, went down south as far as New Mexico, came up again along the east coast back to New York, after nearly nine months.

I don't know how to classify this book. It is not a book of information on America, not is it a study of American culture. It is mainly autobiographical, full of 'I' over a short period of time in relation to some moments, scenes and personalities.

This book was written thirty years ago and I do not know, as I've said at the beginning of this foreword, how far 'dateless-ness' can hold. I do not, for instance, know how many of the friends I mention are still alive or where they are and how many of them are still unseparated. In other ways, too, the country I first visited, has changed. But there are certain things that will endure.

Ultimately, as I've written elsewhere, America and India are profoundly different in attitude and philosophy, though it would be wonderful if they could complement each other's values. Indian philosophy stresses austerity and unencumbered, uncomplicated day-to-day living. America's emphasis, on the other hand, is on material acquisition and the limitless pursuit of prosperity. From childhood, an Indian is brought up on the notion that austerity and a contented life are good, a certain otherworldliness is inculcated through Grandmother's tales, the discourses at the temple hall, and moral books. The American has a robust indifference to eternity. 'Attend church on Sunday and listen to the sermon, but don't bother about the future,' he seems to say. Also, he seems to echo Omar Khayyam's philosophy: 'Dead yesterday and unborn tomorrow, why fret about them if today be sweet ?' He works hard and earnestly, acquires wealth and enjoys life. He has no time to worry about afterlife, only taking care to draw up a proper will and trusting the funeral home to take care of the rest. The Indian in America who is not able to live wholeheartedly on this basis finds himself in a halfway house, he is unable to overcome his conflicts while physically flourishing on American soil.

But to return to the subject of this book. This is not a well-researched historical study of America and its inhabitants, merely a record of first impressions of people and places in that country. It should perhaps be read as a sort of subjective minor history of a country that I love.

Mysore   *R.K. Narayan*
March 1988

MY DATELESS DIARY

1

NEW YORK DAYS

Over a Cup of Coffee

YESTERDAY, at the self-service cafeteria, I made the mistake of waiting for someone to ask what I wanted. Today I know better. You enter the cafeteria, pull out a 'check' (on which prices are punched) from a machine, pick up a tray and spoons, and study the various dishes displayed on the long counter under a glass cover, trying to judge what's what and how far a vegetarian could venture—whether that attractive yellow stuff might not be some prohibited food such as lobster; the men here evidently do not like anyone to stare so long at their display; one of them asks in a surly manner, 'What do you want?' (instead of the ever-polite 'Can I help you?') They are black-haired, hatchet-faced men, possessing a Latin temper perhaps; not the blond, soft-spoken Mayflower descendants. How differently you got through a restaurant-session in Mysore. You took your seat, asked for the morning paper and a glass of water—just to mark time before deciding whether you should have *Masala Dosai* again or *Idli,* or as you generally felt inclined (but resisted) both; but indecision could never be an end in itself, and you devised a further postponement of issues, by asking, when the reading of the paper was over, 'What have you?' A routine question. The waiter would give a quick recital of the day's menu—nothing new or startling, but you enjoyed hearing it all over again. Coming from a civilization used to this pace of life, I felt unequal to the speed of a Broadway Cafeteria. If you hesitated with the tray in hand, you blocked the passage of others and made them silently fret. I fumbled and obstructed only for a day. Today I was as good as my neighbour. I picked up my breakfast and assembled it with deftness, and had on the whole acquired so much smartness that when I approached coffee and was asked, 'Black or white?' 'Neither', I said haughtily. The server looked up rather puzzled. 'What do you mean?' he asked. 'I want it neither black nor white, but brown which ought to be the colour of honest coffee—that's how we make it in South India where devotees of perfection in coffee assemble from all over the world'. He must have thought me crazy, but such leisurely talk is deliberate, like the extra-clutches on the track of a train rolling downhill. I wanted to apply a deliberate counter-action to Broadway's innate rush, just to study the effect. It could prove disastrous as I learnt later about an Indian anthropologist who went to an Automat and nearly paralysed all business while he beamed on every one with, 'Well, my man, how are you?' or 'Where do you come from?' or 'How many children have you?' and so forth. He attempted to make genial conversation with all and sundry, got in everybody's way, fumbled with his purse, asking elaborately: 'Can you give me change please?' at the wrong place, while all the time five-cent coins were rolling out, as from the mint, at the right place. He felt so discouraged at the end of it that he slipped away losing all hope of mastering the art of ordering food in New York; he subsisted for a week on hot chestnut sold at the street corner.

Today I wanted to discourse on the philosophy of brown coffee, but there were other breakfasters, holding their trays, standing behind me inexorably, to secure their coffee and race for a table space. They were too well-mannered to push, but I knew they were fretting inside, each must have had a dozen things to do after breakfast, and how dare I block their business? Still I was in a communicative mood; I smiled at those behind me and said, 'Sorry'. I told the coffee server, 'When you have more time, come to me, I'll tell you all about brown coffee'. I bore away my tray and sat at a secluded table and began to work my way through cornflakes and milk, marmalade and toast, which were to be my main diet for the next ten months. A man in a sports-jacket came over and asked, 'Do you mind?' 'Not at all,' I said. He set his tray on the table, and said, 'I overheard your remark about coffee. You know of any special trick in making it?' God-given opportunity for me to start off a lecture on coffee, its place in South India (in the North they favour tea), its place in our social life, how the darkest condemnation of a family would be the warning uttered at their back, 'Their coffee is awful', how at wedding parties it was the responsibility of the bride's father to produce the best coffee and keep it flowing all day for five hundred at a time; how decoction drawn at the right density, on the addition of fresh warm milk turned from black to sepia, from which ultimately emerged a brown akin to the foaming edge of a river in flood, how the whole thing depended upon one's feeling for quality and eye for colour; and then the ding of sugar, just enough to mitigate the bitterness but without producing sweetness. Coffee making is a task of precision at every stage. I could not help mentioning my mother who has maintained our house-reputation for coffee undimmed for half a century. She selects the right quality of seeds almost subjecting every bean to a severe scrutiny, roasts them slowly over charcoal fire, and knows by the texture and fragrance of the golden smoke emanating from the chinks in the roaster whether the seeds within have turned the right shade and then grinds them into perfect grains; everything has to be right in this business. A daughter-in-law who comes into the family will have to go through several weeks of initiation before she may dare to make the family coffee. 'Three spoons for six persons. Place the powder at the bottom of a stainless steel vessel and pour boiling water over it and then strain it slowly through a piece of cloth'. She is a fanatic and insists on straining coffee only through thin cloth; no power on earth can ever make her change over to a percolator or the more common brass coffee-filter. She considers all such contraptions inimical to her coffee ideals. She gleefully boasted once, 'I have made over a hundred persons throw away their coffee-filters and use the cloth for straining. I shall persuade many more before long. Ultimately coffee-filters should cease to have a market. . .' Such a fanatic, I wondered what her reaction would be to the preposterous question 'White or Black?' She would be infuriated at the very terminology.

'White' coffee actually means, according to her, milk with coffee dash which is administered only to sick persons, black coffee should never be drunk! 'Cream' itself she would object to as it could never help good coffee. Only pure milk, untampered and taken straight from the cow could be a true coffee component.

Ageless in New York

After breakfast I emerged into Broadway. My life in New York had not yet fallen into a routine. I felt free to do what I liked. I could have gone to see my good friend Gilpatric but he was in hospital. It was a pity since my whole visit was planned by him and he was to do so many things for me. He could not be seen for a week more. That left me somewhat uncharted.

I walked up and down, and decided that I might as well spend the week trying to learn something of New York.

*

I passed down 50th street, and sat on one of the benches at Rockefeller Plaza in order to study my diary of engagements. Through a corner of my eye I watched also the goings on around. The Dolphin Fountains and gardens look much more attractive in the 'View-Master' slides. The View-Master has accustomed us to a richer-than-life outlook. People were skating on ice. Young figures clad in coloured jerseys were executing beautiful ballet-like movements. Middle-aged persons skimmed along precariously, held in position by uniformed attendants. Why were aged persons attempting the feat with all that air of daringness? Perhaps they enjoyed the sensation of movement without the lifting of feet or perhaps the spirit of youth bubbled irrepressibly within old frames. The aim might be to ignore age and defy time. With so many facilities in civilization one simply could not afford to grow old. I remember one evening a big hatted cheerful man at the lobby of my hotel, who after dining well stood at the staircase and joked aloud, pointing at all the women coming out of the restaurant, 'Age has no chance in New York,' he announced, 'Look at these women, they are trying to look young with all those hats, ear rings, and paint and girdles—but how long can you cheat age? Not for ever. Even in New York people will have to look their years sooner or later.' He was in a rollicking mood, and all the women walking past him, giggled. He found the women's headgear, in particular, funny. It might sound ungracious to comment on women, but I found myself in agreement with this man's views. Hat designers have persuaded American women to carry on their heads fantastic oddments in felt, fluff, and what not. Some wore hats which had the aesthetic finish of the lid of a marmalade can, some of the women's hats produced the same visual impression as Christy's feltcap of ancient times. I wonder if any one remembers or knows about Christy's caps. At the turn of the century, Christy's caps, were considered in South India at any rate, as the acme of men's fashion. Men shaved the front portion of their heads and grew a tuft at the back and tied it into a knot. The shaved portion of the head was covered with a Christy's cap, which was just half an inch or an inch high, while the tuft stuck out of the rim of the cap at the back. The ensemble was complete with a couple of gem studs on the ear lobes. With the advancing standards of civilized appearance this scheme was given up, and after losing sight of it for years in India, I noticed it now in New York—cap like Christy's, sparkling studs on the ears, tuft at the back; and even the skirts and jackets had a resemblance to the *dhoti* that South Indians wear. I was taken aback to see the abandoned masculine fashion of India adopted by the women of New York as the latest. Another fashion that I noticed was a flat piece resembling a castor-leaf placed on the head of a stylish woman. Peasant women working under a tropical sun, sometimes cover the top of their heads with castor-leaf, which is supposed to keep the brain cool even under the hottest sun. There is every reason for the village women of India to try castor-leaf under a hot sun but what excuse could women of New York have to imitate the fashion (with felt, velvet or whatever it might be) in the middle of the night in Broadway? This was puzzling to me as, to be frank, it lends a touch of irresponsible clownishness to the appearance of women, and seems particularly unsuited to some of the portlier types one notices here and there. Our discussions on fashion was over. The big-hatted man gave me his card and said, 'Any time you visit Texas, you must visit us. Drop me a card ánd my station wagon will pick you up at the rail-station. I enjoy receiving guests, I've a house with 12 guestrooms. You will find the women in our State different; they are not like the women here.'

Guided Men

Most of these men and women were obviously visitors to New York. New York is perhaps the most visitor filled city in the world; unlike Paris or Rome, where the visitors are from other countries, New York is full of Americans themselves, from other States. Later, in every small town or State I found the local resident proudly recollecting his visit to New York last year or five years ago. 'Oh, I can't stand the pace of life there,' he would invariably conclude. But while doing New York, he likes to do it thoroughly. They are all over the place; they form the bulk of the shopping crowd in Fifth Avenue, they follow the guide at the Rockefeller Centre, looking up faithfully at the murals above when his finger points down. They fill the Empire State Building; they cram every inch of available space in Manhattan cruise boats, swarm over the Statue of Liberty, and above all they are the people, if my guess is right, who skate on the ice at Rockefeller Plaza; they are definitely out to enjoy life, every inch of them proclaiming this purpose.

India Behind Glass

Passing down Forty-ninth Street, I suddenly come upon a show window, in which Indian bric-a-brac are displayed. Being Sunday the door is shut but it is studded with mysterious lettering, reading something like G-V-N-T F I-D-I-A TOU-S-T OFF-E. By guessing one might comprehend them as 'The Government of India Tourist Office'—someone has probably been banging on the door to make so many of the letters drop off. At the window the display is almost bare—but for a heavy Thirupathi wooden doll. Beside it stands an ivory figure, which might be anything—a God or a paper-weight. It is tucked far away at the back. The only other Indian article on display here is a brocade and a gaudy picture of a Mogul garden. It leaves me wondering as I have wondered at every tourist office, how this is going to help whom. As though in answer to my query, a passer-by stops to look at the articles in the window. His hat and correct Sunday dress proclaim him to be a week-end visitor to New York. He glues his face to the glass sheet in attempting to study the article inside. I am curious to know what attracts him:

'Can I help you?'

'What's that white stuff? What do you call it?' he asks.

'That's Ivory—'

'What does the figure represent?'

'An Indian God, you know, one of the hundreds of gods in India.'

'I like to have it. Know where I can order such things?'

Immediately I write down for him a few addresses in Mysore, and explain, 'Mysore is in south-western part of India. In its vast jungles elephants flourish, and the figure you see here is carved out of the tusk of an elephant, by craftsmen, who have done nothing else for generations.' It sounds so romantic that I am myself impressed by it. No doubt the American is moved by my description. He confesses: 'My wifelikesthem. She is fond of such things.' He produces his card. He is from Milwaukee; and his card announces him to be the Director of American Association of Bowling.

'What is Bowling?' I ask innocently. He explains, 'It's one of the finest American Institutions,' he says. 'It helps people get a little entertainment, and at the same time just that extra cash everyone needs, you know. More than all it has kept down juvenile delinquency, which is a pressing problem in our country.'

'Why don't you visit my country some day and organize bowling there; we are desperately in need of a lot of diversion as well as extra cash. Juvenile delinquency though not a very big problem yet, may be nipped in the bud, you know. . . Incidentally your wife may buy any quantity of those ivory figures in the bazaars. . .'

He is impressed with my sales-talk and has promised to plan a visit to India.

Gandhi Land

Consulting my pocket book walked down E68 Street, looking for a doctor from India, whose address had been given to me at London. People give us addresses for a variety of reasons. Sometimes it's purely mercenary—some will want us to carry pickles and spices from India to their kith and kin abroad. Apart from the utilitarian motive quite a number of persons offer the addresses of persons known to them, I am sure, in order to be helpful to a man going into strange lands: 'If you see so and so, he'll give you the maximum assistance.' I didn't have the heart to confess that my friend Gil's help was quite adequate for me officially, personally, and in every conceivable way. I had accepted all the introductions unthinkingly. Now I suddenly asked myself, 'Why should I see this doctor?' There was no logical answer to it. I didn't come ten thousand miles to see an unknown Indian doctor. I dropped the idea of seeing him, but going down to its very end, I acquired a working knowledge of 68th Street.

Saw a sub-way opening at the end of the street, and went down. Held out a coin through the window as I saw others do and received back, what I took to be two coins but actually a dime and a token. I asked where it'd take me. The man at the window asked:

'Where do you want to go?'

'Anywhere.'

'Up-town or down-town?'

I was not sufficiently educated yet to know what up or down-town meant. So I said, 'I just want to look around.' He looked sickened by my vagueness and aimlessness, and spurned to comment further. I slipped in the token as others did, turned the stile and jumped into a train. Whether it was down or up—I'd no idea. Everybody was getting out of the train all the way. I was the only passenger when the train reached its terminus. I got out, and wandered through a park full of mighty trees with leaves changing colour—one of the finest sights of New York in this season. Fine sunshine. Youngsters in bright sweaters were playing a game. Walked down a road admiring a row of new villas, and went back to my starting point. Felt hungry and slipped into a shop and asked for food, explaining that I was a vegetarian. I uttered the word 'Vegetarian' with the greatest caution since it stirred people in all unexpected ways; and dismayed them as if I had said I was a 'Man-eater'. So I generally softened the blow by asking 'Can you give me a lunch, please?'

'Yes'.

'But, you know, I don't eat meat.'

'Oh, that doesn't bother me, I can give you fish.'

'No fish, please.'

'I can give you, perhaps, an omelette?'

'No eggs please I don't eat fish, fowl, or meat.' Before he or she looked completely shattered, I added in a sort of constructive way, 'May be you could fix me a meal with toast, cheese, fruit, yogurt, rice, carrot and tomato?'

'Oh, yes', and they proceeded to give me my food, without any more difficulty. Someone might occasionally ask, 'Why are you a vegetarian?'

'I don't know. Have never been anything else'.

'Are you a vegetarian by conviction or religion?'

'I am a born-vegetarian. I cannot eat anything except rice, greens, and dairy produce.'

'Extraordinary! Wonder that you are alive.'

I ordered my lunch. The lady bustled about. She was kindly, interested, and sympathetic, and said, 'I'll fix it, don't worry', and gave me bread and coffee, and apple pudding. When they learnt that I was a writer from India, they gathered around me. They held me as a show-piece presenting me to their customers coming in for cigarettes and ice-cream. The woman's husband, an old man, came forward and said, 'I like Gandhi, but Nehru is not like Gandhi, am I right?'

'No, you are wrong,' I said.

'Nehru is friendly to the Communists, isn't he?'

'No, if you read the Indian papers you would understand his views better.'

'Oh, I don't know. Anyway, Gandhi was great. I've tried to read everything about him.'

Another young man who worked in an automobile firm in Manhattan and came here every week-end to visit his grandmother at a nursing home, joined us and added,

'Gandhi was a sturdy man. What a strong man was he!'

'But he weighed only ninety pounds,' I added.

The talk was all about Gandhi and his life. They listened to my description of the Mahatma with interest, and gasped with surprise at my description of the mighty congregations at his prayer meetings. They were very happy and proud that I should have come all the way from Manhattan to Bronx, just to see the place—which seemed to them an impossible feat—as city-dwellers live and die rigidly within their own orbits. They were more impressed with my visiting Bronx than my coming all the way from the India. Children were dropping in for ice cream and milk shakes, pausing to listen to my talk. When I rose to leave, the old man came forward to shake my hand, really proud to have seen a man from 'Gandhiland'.

On my way back, got in and out of all wrong buses. Got out of a bus which terminated at the University Avenue. No bus seemed to go in my direction. North, South, East and West looked confusing near the University Avenue. Finally, went down the steps of a subway, to ask for direction at the ticket-window. Found a communicative American at the ticket-window.

'Down-town, get off at 50th Street change to a local to 50th Street and walk a block.' He peered at me through the small window and asked,'From India?'

'Yes.'

'What do you think of Nehru?' he asked straight away. Second time someone was asking about Nehru.

'Fine man,' I said.

'Is he good?' he asked.

'In every way,' I said although I was talking so confidently about one whom I'd never met. He merely said, 'Just wanted to know that is all.'

Portugueseness

At the hotel I phoned for the service of an electrician, something having gone wrong with my reading lamp. A heavy man in a blue overall knocked on my door. He examined the light, pulled out its wires, and looked worried as he said, 'Someone has badly done this.' He looked like a detective sitting over a corpse. I hoped that he didn't imply that I had tampered with it. 'I will fix it,' he said with a touch of menace in his voice, 'But it must be righted here first,' he said, obscurely tapping his head. I expressed agreement with all his views because he smelt faintly of alcohol. He added, 'Don't talk to me if you don't want to; I must not be seen talking to you; they may fire me.'

'Sure, you won't tell them?'

'No, I promise,' I said.

'It's good to talk to you,' he said, 'I know Polish, Portuguese, Spanish and English—two and two, four languages,' he said holding up four fingers.

'But I hope your Polish etc. are better than your English,' I said truthfully.

'Yes, yes, sure,' he said. 'I know Spanish well,' and added, 'You know Spanish?'

'No. . .'

'Portuguese?'

'No. . .'

'But you are Portuguese, aren't you'?

'No. . .'

'You look like Portuguese. You are very much a Portuguese,' he repeated obstinately.

I wanted to look into a mirror and verify. He seemed relieved to know that I was not a Portuguese, and said with disgust, 'I have travelled. But in South America they speak no Spanish, only Portuguese: they call it Spanish. Bút it's no Spanish, but Portuguese.'

'What a pity!' I said, although it was all the same to me.

'Sure you don't know Portuguese?' he asked and after I reaffirmed my non-Portugueseness, he asked,

'Where do you belong?'

'India.'

He repeated, 'India! never heard of it.' He remained in thought for a while and said,

'Say it again?. . . where is it? Funny! Sounds familiar,' he said,

'Mention a place there, may be I've been there in my ship—but—' he tapped his head woefully, 'Mention a place.'
I said, 'Madras. . .'
'No, never heard of it, mention another.'
'Delhi.'
'No, first time I hear the name.'
'Calcutta,' I said.
'No such place,' he replied shaking his head. 'Bombay.'
'Ah, Bombay! sounds like a place I know. Is it India? Is it a port? I am sure I must have been there, but you know I was the sort that never went ashore. My business was in the engine room and there I stayed. I went round the world for thirty years but never went ashore anywhere, until I gave up service and landed in New York.' Before leaving he tore off the lamp from its holder and took it with him, promising, 'You'll see a new lamp on your bed when you come home tonight.' He made a request before passing out of the door, 'If you meet them down there', indicating a vast horde of managers and employers, 'Tell them your engineer is a good guy, that'll help me.'

Missing Letters Dropped

After all found the India Tourist Office open and walked in. A couple of young men in the office downstairs got quite a thrill out of meeting me and instantly proposed that I should address the Indian Students Association at New York. Warded off the proposal gently since I loathe all lectures and hope to survive the American visit without adding my voice to the babble around. The boss of this establishment proved to be a happy, friendly soul, who immediately sent up a phone call to the Indian Consul and tried to involve me in a forthcoming party there in honour of the Indonesian Tax Commission or some such highly eclectic body. Out of consideration for his kind-hearted effort, I simulated a provincial enthusiasm for the party, but in a strictly non-committal way. Seeing him at close quarters I found it impossible to be critical of his Tourist Office. Even the missing letters on the door did not seem to matter : I never mentioned it, leaving the rectification of such errors to the gods.

Publishers

Being published by a University Press is a distinction no doubt, but a disadvantage commercially speaking. Booksellers, who are an inevitable link between an author and his public will not stock a university publication. You may print on the cover of your book, as boldly as you will, that it is a work of fiction, guaranteed not to enlighten, bore, or instruct, quoting all the reviews, but still the book-seller will have his misgivings when he sees a university imprint. He has a fear that under the jacket of fiction someone is attempting to sell him a heavily-loaded Ph.D. thesis.

For nearly twenty years I managed without an American publisher, and year after year my English agent reported that the time was not ripe yet. I accepted it as an inevitable state of affairs until around 1953, the late Lyle Blair became Director of Michigan State University Press, and the first thing he did was to wire us an offer to publish all my books. He was a man, though we had never met, of tremendous personal enthusiasm for my writing; he used to publish my books in England, and in Europe. He was the first publisher to bring out an English book in Europe after the war, and that was my *English Teacher* printed in Vienna in the Guild Edition. I've always felt that if Lyle Blair were at the head of a Law Publishing firm, he'd still find an excuse to reprint one of my novels in their series. He published five of my books within a period of eighteen months. The reviews were always favourable, but unfortunately as he himself confessed in his note to *Swami and Friends,* the sales were poor, but he was still prepared to go on with the publications, unmindful of the results. When arrived in New York, the late Harvey Breit, my good friend, (then) of the *New York Times,* made it his mission to find me a New York publisher purely for commercial reasons; he also took the responsibility of smoothening out the human side of it with Lyle Blair, who was then away in Australia.

Harvey Breit telephoned me a list of publishers to see. He had made appointments for me, morning and afternoon so that I should meet a new publisher every two hours. After breakfast one morning, I started out and beginning with Viking at 625

Madison, I worked my way up and down strictly on a schedule. After seeing all of them I was to decide who was to publish me. There was a touch of unreal ease about it. I had really no notion what I should say to them since I had no manuscript to offer. I went through it because it was going to be fun knowing the publishers of New York. I did not think anyone would seriously bother about me. All my life I was used only to publishers who could not be moved, and who were wary and on the defensive when they met a writer. But here were men who did not believe in being cautious or diplomatic and who plainly stated within ten minutes of our meeting that they would like to be my publishers. It's good for an author to feel wanted. It became harder to choose as I saw more and more of them. I was impressed with all the men I met. Myer, Editor of Scribners, who seemed so full of refinement and high values, Harold Strauss of Knopf, whose wonderful conversation held me spell-bound, James Laughlin himself of New Directions an old friend since an evening long ago he had walked into my Mysore home (as I was struggling to produce my Sunday article for a paper), after flying from Bombay to Coimbatore and motoring a hundred miles from Ooty. Saxe Commins of Random House, who admitted total ignorance of anything I wrote but still wanted to try me, and whose talk of Einstein and Gandhi fascinated me; or Storer Lunt, genial, warm and extraordinarily human, with whom I had an unforgettable dinner at a restaurant and then a drive around New York one night. He spoke of New York with love and excitement and in the three hour drive with him, I saw the subtle beauty of this City, especially at night when its buildings are lit and its waters scintillate, and the sky-scraping windows are aglow. Simon Bessie of Harpers, one of the liveliest minds, who quoted from my novel *Waiting for the Mahatma*. How could I make a choice, when all of them were so good and friendly? I despaired of being able to choose, and requested Harvey Breit to cancel a few other names he had had on his list.

Reminiscential Dog-lover

To the East River side just to investigate this part of New

York. Automobiles were speeding off south and north as if in a delirium. I got into a wrong track and then into a carving tunnel prohibited to pedestrians. I had had no idea of the prohibition; but I noticed passing motorists throwing curious glance at me. Later emerging from the tunnel I read the sign outside, *'Pedestrians prohibited'*. While in the tunnel I had to stand for nearly an hour pressing myself close to the wall, with automobiles speeding within half a foot of me, and a gust of wind heating me in the face each time a car passed. I feared that if an extra-fat model came along, it'd plaster me to the wall. Or at least, I feared, I might never leave the spot again, until I dropped down through fatigue and they picked me up and carried my famished self—a martyr to no nobler cause than pedestrianism.

It was a relief to come into the open, under the open skies again. I climbed a pedestrian's overbridge in order to take in uninterrupted the beauty of the river, barges and boats cruising along, the evening sky, and the mighty bridge spanning the river. From my eminence, I could watch with detachment the traffic flow by, long cars, longer cars and still longer cars in multicolours. In any other country's traffic, there'd be a mixture of long cars and not so long cars and (in our own country) bullock carts, stray cattle thrown in, but here in New York, there was a continuous parade of elongated vehicles— going in three layers or four—on the bridge, below the bridge, on the road, over the road—up and down. As I stood watching, an old man came up the steps of pedestrian bridge leading two dogs— a venerable man, with a handsome face and god-given wrinkles and blue-eyes. One of his dogs was an Alsatian and the other was a very short, puny indistinct variety. We were the only two on the bridge. Standing in this eminence, we could afford to take a lenient view of the excited traffic below.'Won't bite?' I asked as an opening. 'Oh no, just playful you know. Wants to play, but if I unchain him, I will have to pay a fine of twenty-five dollars. Can't afford it?'

'You love dogs?' I asked.

Such questions, however banal, have the effect of bringing humanity closer. 'Oh, dogs mean everything to me,' he said. 'I had a Great Dane once, so high', I said recollecting Sheba, black and white, so beautiful and gentle and big that she was often mistaken for a heifer. He came closer and told me about dogs, their pedigrees, the best years of their lives and so on. 'Six is the best year of a dog's life, but at ten he is like me; he likes to curl up and sleep all the time. What's the use? He's then a dog only in appearance. Until he is two he is no good as a dog either. I'd another one—.' More about dogs and then he asked me about myself and India. 'Is it a fact that you have a population—over 400 million, Oh God, what a number, and most of them die of starvation?' His view was a limited granary and a stampede by a mass of humanity for it. He wanted to know what we did for food. 'You have pigs, cattle and poultry—yes? Then what's the trouble? How is the winter there?'

'In most parts of the country—the sharpest winter day is like what we have in New York now,' I said. He was astonished; and started off on his weather experience. He told me about himself: A Swede who had come with his father as a boy of fifteen, fifty years ago. Served as a valet in the household of a famous chain-store magnate and travelled widely in all the states, 'When he died his daughter inherited the business and married an Italian count, who didn't even know English—and let me tell you a secret; he already had two children and a wife, but married again for money. . . Money is everything still. Money speaks: Do you think people elect?. . . It's money which decides to have someone there and someone not there. . . that's all. . . I'm voting for whosoever will prevent atom bombs exploding in the seas and poisoning the fish I eat . . . Anyway why should there be atom bombs?. . See, all this building destroyed and wounded children mean nothing to a man bombing from the air—so I was told by a man who had been a pilot in the war. He took an abstract view of destruction and death while releasing his bombs. War is unnecessary, there should be no war. You are an Indian, I am from Sweden; are we not getting along now? We are all one; no need to fight even if we are all different. . . Come to Sweden some time; Oh, when I think of Stockholm. . . I want to go back and die there, but my wife loves her sister, who lives in Long Island, and won't part from her. We've no children, but these dogs I love. Going down the riverside? 'Oh no, you can't at this hour. Listen to my advice; there are bums and dope-fiends who will assault and rob you. Don't go down; if you live in Broadway you should turn back and come along with me, and take the bus. I've lived in this area for 50 years. For 30 years I lived over there in a house on Second Avenue. In those days, you did not have sky-scrapers. . . Only a few old houses and open spaces and buses were parked right here where you see this huge building twenty-stories high with its elevator and all. It's all wonderful change now. . . All these places belonged to Rockefeller once, and he gave them away. After the 1914 war I saw respectable persons queuing for bread and white-collared men sleeping on newspaper in the subway. Bad times: factories closed and all kinds of things happened. . . And a war came up and things picked up. But war is bad. . . When you go to Sweden, don't miss Stockholm, that's my place. I like to talk to people. It's so good to have someone to talk to. Nowadays nobody finds the time to stand and talk. Thank you very much indeed and God bless you. . . Get into this bus; Good bye. It'll take you to your hotel.'

Mrs X

Awakened by the telephone, emerge from the mists of sleep and stretch out my hand for the receiver, but it's at the foot of my bed. I hide my head under the blanket again in the hope that the telephone would cease, but it is insistent. I'm not destined to sleep. Like Macbeth I shall sleep no more.

'May I know who is speaking?'

'I am Mrs. . . I want to ask you. . .'

'Who did you say?'

'You remember we met the other night at J's home where you had come to dinner.' I did not think I should pursue this research anymore. Not in a clear condition of mind. I could perhaps sort it out later.

'Yes, yes, what can I do for you?'

'You see, the psychic portions in your 'Grateful to Life and Death', *(The English Teacher)* interested me, I want to ask a few questions.'

'Go ahead.'

'Is it all a fact? I am eager to know whether it's all fact or fiction.'

I could not catch much of her speech on the phone.

She had borrowed J's copy of *The English Teacher* and read it. 'I want to meet you. Could you come for dinner on Tuesday?'

'Yes,' I said to end the conversation as it was becoming too metaphysical and obscure.

Later I tried to recollect who she might be. It'd been a short notice dinner at J's a few evenings before. I had called on him at his office earlier in the evening and he could give his wife only an hour's notice for preparing a suitable dinner for me. He had also invited a few others to join us after dinner. It'd been an enjoyable party, but for the harrowing thought that perhaps my hosts, out of consideration for me, were starving themselves on rice and greens, adopting for the moment my own diet. The others at the party were: the editor of a home magazine, a young man working in Burma on a Ford Foundation assignment, editor of a highbrow review, and a lady who came with him and whom I (mis) took to be his wife. This was the lady telephoning me now. This lady, I recollected, had been firing off all through the evening a number of questions on idol worship, symbolism and Gandhi and it was difficult for me to answer them because I could not be sure whether she was trying the Socratic method or whether she genuinely sought answers to her questions; her husband's (as I took him to be at the time) English I could not follow. He was a Russian, and spoke a sort of Russian-English, in a sort of through-the-pipe-drawl; he had a rough, authoritative style of speech in a low growling pitch, and was too positive-minded and intimidating.

Luckily I didn't have to bear this trial too long. At about ten o'clock Santha, her husband Faubion Bowers, and Donald Keene, (head of the Japanese section at Columbia), entered, sat down on the carpet since all the chairs were occupied and commanded all the rest to cease talking so that the conversation might be all about *The English Teacher* which they had just read.

*

The telephone woke me up again this morning.

Mrs X again. 'I'd like to see you sometime today. What time are you free?'

'We are meeting at your home tomorrow, aren't we?' I said.

'Yes, but I want to see you today at your place. . . What time are you free?'

'Two o'clock,' I said without a thought, unable to turn the leaves of my little engagement diary with one hand, while the other held the telephone.

'What's your time?' I asked. Thus do I exploit all those who call me in the morning since I do not possess a watch.

'Nine-thirty,' she said and I decided not to go back to bed. I made myself a cup of instant coffee with hot water from the bathroom tap. It was eleven o'clock when I emerged from my room. Felt extremely reluctant to visit the cafeteria and so skipped breakfast, not feeling well enough to bear the smell of carrot in that place. Walked down to E 65 to call on Mrs Gilpatric intending to take only five minutes of her time in order to enquire about her husband's health, but I stayed on. We had so much to talk about, she knew Mysore and its people, and we had common subjects for a whole day's talk, and so I didn't notice the time passing. When I started back for my hotel, I glanced at the clock on a wayside shop, 1.30 p.m. At 2 p.m. Mrs X would be at my hotel. This was going to leave me no time for lunch. While hurrying along to meet Mrs X, at a cross-road, encountered the lady whose name I never caught at Harvey's party the other evening, but who sat beside me and chatted for a whole hour. Before leaving she had said, 'I should not monopolize you. Will you call me sometime to say when you will be free? I like to take you round to visit some of our book-shops.' Now she met me at the corner of Madison Avenue, and said, 'Hallo, I expect your telephone call tomorrow morning, remember,' and passed on with a friendly smile. I was on the point of confessing that unless I knew her name I could not call her on the phone; but I could not bring myself up to it. I had let her assume too long that I knew her. She had even shouted her telephone number to me over the din of the party that evening, but I'd forgotten it.

Mrs X—was waiting for me at the hotel lounge. I was fifteen

minutes late. She carried a huge bunch of red flowers in her hand. She followed me to my room, and bustled about to find a place for the flowers.

'Have you a vase?' She asked.

'I'll call for one, meanwhile, let me keep them in the sink.' I took charge of the flower, all the time wanting to burst out:

'Oh Lady, I crave for lunch
Not bloom in a bunch,'

'How much time have you for me?' she asked. I looked through my pocket diary.

'Half an hour perhaps,' I said. 'I have an engagement at the N.B.C.at three.'

She said, 'After hearing Faubion speak about it, I borrowed J's copy of *Grateful toLifeand Death* and read it. It has made me feel that we have a common experience. I too lost someone dear to me. He was my friend, an obstetrician who helped me deliver my baby about a year ago. I loved him. There was profound understanding between us; he meant everything to me. Ten days after my baby was born he died in a motor accident. I was convalescing in our Long Island home—it is a large house but we do not live there but only in a rented flat in New York for the sake of my husband's business and my daughter's school. By the way, if you need a quiet place for writing, please go up and stay there whenever you like and as long as you like.'

'You were telling me about your doctor,' I said bringing her back to the main subject.

'Yes, during that period of convalescing I was rather sensitive, I suppose. My friend said good-bye to me, gave me some routine instructions, and started out on a long drive one day. I felt all along that I might probably never see him again. Within an hour of our parting I learnt that his car had skidded. I was rather sensitive and felt his spirit hovering near me, I felt that he was reproaching me for not stopping him from going out that day when I knew all along that he would never return. I might probably have saved him with a word. Why did I not say it? I am anxious to communicate with his spirit. Do you think it will be possible? I feel psychically sensitive.' 'I don't want to do anything,' she said, 'that may seem odd and eccentric in the American eye. I feel inclined to fast once a fortnight and I feel psychically sensitive. I go to my church and meditate regularly. . . Still I feel there must be a technique. Please tell me what I should do to develop myself fully. I live comfortably. I love my husband. I love my children. They are all very good to me. I write, I paint, I do various things, still I feel there is something else that I should do. I want your help. Your book tells me that you know about these things.'

I didn't know what to say. At no time did I think that my book, however close it might be to my own life and outlook, would ever involve me in a practical problem. I wanted to think over it. I didn't like to say anything light or irresponsible. She seemed earnest and greatly troubled in mind, and at the same time high-strung; any severe concentration or psychic effort, I felt, might upset her. I told her,

'I will try and answer your question when we meet on Tuesday.'

'Many thanks. Dinner will be at six-thirty. Could you come at five-thirty? My husband and children will be home at six, and I shall want half an hour's talk with you before we settle down to dinner.'

'Yes, I will try.'

'I don't want others to take me to be eccentric you know,' she said. She added, 'The other day at J's house you saw a millionaire's flat. You should also see how an ordinary, common American family lives. We are not rich. We work hard to make both ends meet. You should see us. That's why I am inviting you to our house. . . Well, another thing. My friend's name was. . .' She wrote it down for me on a piece of paper. If you manage to contact his spirit, tell me what he says. Tell me if he has any message for me. . . See those flowers, he was fond of red. That's why I have got them here. I am sure if you keep those flowers with you, you will be able to tell me something.'

Super-Guide

Finished my lunch at four-thirty which is nearer the American dinner time, and hurried along to the National Broadcasting Corporation studios at the Rockefeller Centre. An efficient guide took us along: he was witty, smart, familiar, factual, as he took us through room after room, and showed us with a good deal of explanation a few persons miming beyond a sheet-glass; and he pointed out elementary things such as boom, camera, monitor, etc. He behaved like a cheerful elementary school teacher taking his children through a museum. We were an assorted crowd : men, women and children, had converged here from the forty-eight states, and of course, like me on their first visit. The guide's smartness, kindliness, elaborate speech and ready wit got on my nerves because it was so well-practised; his smooth speech, I suddenly realised, took the place of actual exhibits; after walking along endless corridors and up and down flights of steps, one realised that one had finally seen only charts and dummies and heard the guide's lectures on the technicalities of television.He reminded me of the chief character in my new novel,—a tourist guide who conjured history and archaeology out of thin air. I suddenly recollected the amusing sight of visitors streaming along the gardens of Gemini Studio in Madras behind a Public Relations Officer. 'This is the cutting room, that is the laboratory,' he would say indicating the exteriors of various sections, never showing them anything really, while the crowd followed patiently, hoping till the last second to get a peep at a star or a scene being shot. I couldn't stand it any more. Suddenly I slipped away from the crowd and strode down the corridors, saying 'Excuse me,' to people standing in the way, and everyone here thinking everyone else an executive going in a hurry, made way. I merged with a crowd at the elevator, who had completed their travails and were being seen off by their guide.

Two Tickets or None

I owed my visit to the National Broadcasting Corporation to that energetic soul Miss Roser of Anta (American National Theatre and Academy). I had met her at her Broadway office in her little cubicle beyond the receptionist, surrounded with masks and costumes. She was an extremely active person. Theatre organization was the very breath of her life. She took immediate charge of anyone who wanted to see the stage or understand its working in America. The first thing she did on our meeting was to make me write down my name phonetically and rehearse her in pronouncing it. She was interested in India and had a fantastically remote, unguessable link with it. She confessed that she had done the part of Shakuntala when Kalidasa's play was staged, I don't remember where, years and years before, and she confessed that it was one of her proudest memories. Within half an hour of meeting me, she picked up her telephone and fixed a number of appointments for me to watch rehearsals, plays, meet theatrical men and so forth. She promised also to give me a series of introductions so that I might contact theatre men in every corner of the country. She proved too fast for me, giving me no time to think and reply; Wednesday afternoon Anta Theatre, Thursday 7.30 Carnegie's Hall 'Johnny Jhonson', Friday Television studios and so on and on. She would suddenly take the telephone and say, 'Hallo, this is Roser of Anta speaking. You have been so good to us at other times that I am tempted to trouble you again now. You see the problem is I have now sitting here right before me a distinguished gentleman from India who has come on a Rockefeller to study the theatre movement in this country. He wants to see a rehearsal. . . I would appreciate your help—all right I'll hold on, tell me your time and date. . . Yes, certainly he is a distinguished visitor from India interested in the theatre of course.' She would cover the mouthpiece with her palm at this stage and plead, 'Really, do you realize I know nothing about you? Please sympathise with me and give me a note about yourself so that I may tell these folk the truth about you.' She would then resume her telephone conversation and tell me finally:

'Go to such and such theatre, and mention your name at the box office and they will have two tickets for you.'

'Two? Why two tickets?'

'It is always so. Two tickets or none, is an inflexible principle in this country.'

Rain and Reason

The last day of October looks like the last day of the world with its unceasing rain since the morning. I get drenched before reaching the Rockefeller Building four blocks off. Added to the rain a taxi splashes up all the road water over me, drenching me up to my ears. Mr. July (of the Foundation) must be aghast at the picture I present, and suggests that I return to my room and change. Of course, I see no point in changing, since I have to be moving about and surely get drenched again. My tour programme is finalized. I shall leave New York in a couple of days.

Next I have to go to the Viking Press. Vikings are entering a practical phase in tackling me. A telegram came to my hotel last evening inviting me to lunch.

I could easily walk there from the Rockefeller Centre, but it is wet outside, and I feel I shall be wise in taking a cab. And so I stand on Fifth Avenue watching taxis dash past. After half an hour's gesticulation I am able to stop one. When I reach Viking the meter shows 35 cents. Give the driver fifty cents. He remarks, 'Big nickel! I can build a house with it, I suppose!' I don't know why he says it or what he means. The sight of coins provokes taxi drivers in strange, unexpected ways.

Hour of Decision

Keith Jennison introduces me to Harold Guinzburg, the President of the firm, who at once refers to Graham Greene for whom he has admiration as an author and affection as a person, and concludes, 'Graham is our author, and you will be in good company. I am sure you will be happy with us.' I am hesitant, having misgivings about my ability to face a commitment. There is no rational basis for this hesitation since it is a first-rate firm and their approach to me is also first-rate. But I think I like to postpone a decision, because it is so much easier. We adjourn to a nearby restaurant for lunch, dashing across in the rain and hopping from awning to awning, 'Somehow, I will always, from now on,' wrote Keith Jennison to me later, 'associate the rainiest days in New York with you. The afternoon we officially became your publishers was wet enough to have made me feel like a fish ever since,' which was appropriate since the novel I was planning but despaired of writing had much to do with rain.* At the restaurant I made no announcement regarding my preferences but quietly ordered a vegetable plate (during my subsequent visits to this restaurant the waiter fetched a vegetable plate at the sight of me). The luncheon party consisted of Keith and a couple of others from the office. We sat at the table talking and eating till three in the afternoon and on going back to his office Keith seated me in a chair opposite him, and said point-blank,

'Have you made up your mind about a publisher?'

'No,' I said, undecided as ever.

'You started with us, and after one round of visiting the publishers, you are back, the cycle is complete now. We like to publish your books. We shall be glad to sign a contract with you and give you an advance on your next book. Have you any reason why you should not immediately say—yes?'

'How are you sure of my next novel?'

This was not a mere point of argument but a real fear. I am never sure of my book at any stage. I dread any commitment ahead. 'We'll take the risk, that is all,' said Jennison. 'We do have faith in you as a writer from our knowledge of your books, and we hope what you write will be O.K., but if something goes wrong we won't hold you responsible, it is a part of the risk of a publisher's business.'

'I said, I may not like to take any money in advance before I write my book.' 'As you wish. But you are going about travelling, all that may be expensive, and if you need funds at any time, just let us know...'

Very gentle and roundabout reference to money.

I am impressed with their delicacy. Money should always be a roundabout hinted at subject between friends, only then is it possible to maintain the dignity of human relations. Finally Jennison bursts out, 'After all this is your agent's business, let him speak to us about it.' I ask for another day to remain undecided and leave.

---

* *The Guide*, published by Viking in 1958

Charred Halloween

Mrs X stands at her doorway watching the street. She is delighted to see me although I'm half an hour late for the engagement. I am happy to see her 'average American home'. They live on the ground floor, the furnishing is almost Indian in its simplicity. I see no one yet around. She shows me a seat and immediately asks,

'What have you to tell me? Did those flowers give you any message?'

I have to explain to her that occult experience cannot be ordered, and then she asks,

'What about my problem? Have you a solution for me?'

'Don't attempt any concentration, meditation, or any such activity for at least six months. Just allow your mind to be restful, that is all I have to say. In due course if you are destined to have a new experience it will come to you. You cannot seek it by force.' I am sorry to sound so heavy and pontifical, but this is the only way in which I can caution her against straining her mind. As she opens her mouth to ask something more a sudden charred smell fills the air. 'Oh, dear, I have let those halloween seeds get charred!' It is Halloween time and pumpkin seeds were being roasted for the children according to the custom on this day. The lady put them on the oven and came down to the street to look for me and forgot about them. Now the pumpkin seeds have turned into carbon and fill the kitchen and the house with acrid smoke. Her daughter comes running into the kitchen, sees the charred seeds and looks sad, 'You have done this mummy!' The girl is nearly in tears. Mrs X apologizes to her. It brings in her husband also from another room. I realize what a blunder I had almost committed. I had all along treated her as the wife of that grumpy intellectual editor, just because they happened to arrive together at J's house, the other evening. Here the real husband is different. However, it has been a purely subjective blunder and hurt no one. We sit down to dinner. It is a nice happy family centring round a chubby baby with four teeth. The husband is in business. Over dinner he asks, as everyone does here, about Gandhi, Nehru, and India in general, and about my writing. The dinner is fine but I am as ever bothered by the thought that perhaps my hosts were starving themselves for the sake of courtesy, on a meal of avacado, carrot and apple. I am delighted to note that Mrs X gives no sign in her husband's presence of her psychic and philosophical trials. Her husband is good enough to drive me back to my hotel at night. I like him, he is a level-headed, hardworking business man, with a modicum of information on all matters. There is no reason to doubt his devotion to her or her devotion to him. Yet the wife has secret pressures on her mind. I only hope she will not harass him with her artistic, psychic, and other angularities, all of which he may find particularly baffling.

Pride and Prejudice

Americans like to know how far they are being liked by others. They have a trembling anxiety lest they should be thought of badly. We Indians are more hardened, having been appreciated, understood, misunderstood, represented, misrepresented, rated, and over-rated from time immemorial both in factual account and in fiction; we take it as a matter of routine to be roused to indignation when we find India attacked and create quite a scene but it is never more than a passing indignation, nor do we honour our detractors by saying that we are pained by such and such comments. We stop bothering about an unjust, cantankerous book, the moment its sales go up as a consequence of public protest; it is different with Americans, who seem to feel genuinely pained by ill-informed criticism. I came across quite a number of Americans who personally loved Graham Greene's writing but could not bring themselves to reading *The Quiet American* for fear that it might upset them. Americans do not mind others enjoying themselves moderately at their expense, poking fun at their speech, habits, prosperity and gadgets, as most English writers have done since the time of Dickens. Americans have always displayed great hospitality to a writer or lecturer who would be humorous at their expense; but they hate to be hated, although in order to put you at ease, your perfect host will indulge in a mild disparagement of American habits, gadgets, or the T.V.

Within the country itself there are small prides and prejudices which one must fully appreciate if one is to understand the country and its people. The test of a visitor's understanding is his sharing of local prejudices.

There is a marked difference of view between North and South and between East and West as anywhere else in the world. To a Southerner the rest of the United States is an immature undeveloped country, a sort of geographical appendage, the New Englander is proud of his heritage of sober English qualities and the beauty of his landscape, the West Coast is an extremely proud country, their weather, their mountains, roses, grapes and tomatoes are ever a source of continuous pride and they like to hear someone say, 'Oh, I can't stand the pace of New York or its weather. What a relief to be here!' There is no great harm done in letting people cherish their prejudices and even sharing them yourself as long as you don't air your views in a family gathering where, as it often happens, New England and California or Mid-west and Oklahoma may be united in matrimony, when polite conversation on prejudices will have to be carried on with circumspection.

*

It's raining hard, and so reach Mrs Dorothy Norman's house at Seventieth Street in a damp state for tea. It's an impressive house in the heart of Manhattan, filled with pictures, images, manuscripts and books—right from the street door all the way along the staircase to the halls upstairs. Looks like an art gallery. Dorothy Norman had made tea and tit-bits, and we sit over-looking her garden beyond the french window, and talk of a hundred things; philosophy, Gandhi, religion, Gita, and the universality of human types, and ancient Indian handicrafts. She has been in India and knows her India. She says that she likes South India more than the North, a very pleasing thing to hear, as pleasing as it'll be for a North Indian to be told that Madras is detestable in everyway.

(Gil said yesterday that he preferred Mysore to Bangalore—excellent sentiment, sir, the finest test of a visitor's understanding as we have already seen, is his participation in local prejudices). We discuss at length the effect of architecture and sculpture on the temper of a pupil and their social life as seen in old South Indian temples—with their colonnades, corridors and halls and sky-scraping towers. She asks me to say what characteristics, according to my understanding, mark off an average American from an Indian. I cannot help confessing, 'I definitely feel man to man, an average American is totally materialistic in the best sense of the term, work, wages, good wife, and good life—are all his main interests; while an Indian will be bothering about the next life also in addition to all this.'

*

At the Indian restaurant, a new American waiter in attendance at dinner. I feel rather apologetic about ordering *a la carte* rice and yogurt, and explain 'You know, we in India, live on rice and yogurt!' He replies, the gentle considerate soul, 'Why not, Sir? Excellent thing. I myself try and take a lot of rice and yogurt whenever I can'. So that puts a stamp of absolute correctitude on the whole issue.

Limp Biscuits

I must have been observing fantastic timings today. When I woke up and made myself coffee, I did not ask for time at the telephone (as I generally do); but sat down and wrote letters, and then asked for the time; came the answer,

'Twenty past three, sir.'

'Thank you,' I said trying not to look shocked.

I had been under the impression that it was noon. It was getting beyond a joke, my timeless existence in the heart of New York! I decided to buy a watch at once (not pursued, really), I missed both breakfast and lunch. I hurried out for a snack at 4 o'clock and then to fulfil a tea at 5 p.m. Still another day come and nearly gone and I have had no time again for anything—seeing Gil or to say 'how do you do?' to Harvey or to buy a shirt, all of which I had proposed to do. This lack of time was getting to be a nightmare and I decided to do something about it as soon as I could find the time for it. The tea proved a most wasteful engagement one could ever accept. I'd to search for the house at the back of beyond down-town area. Had to change buses twice, once legitimately and once through a blunder, and then had to explore the alleys for number 240A. Added to it was a persistent drizzle. Finally found a household perched on a staircase landing, with the lady of the house very loud and casual. Perhaps when they invite you to tea they expect you to drink Martini; when I was offered and declined liquor, they provided me a tea that tasted like rain-water flowing down the roof tile; and to go with it was biscuit that had the look of Salvador Dali's 'Limp Watch'. My host, I realized, welcomed visitors, because he wanted an audience for his incessant chatter at high speed! I suddenly realized that it was a mad evening, with an engagement that I ought to have waived with grace and dignity. Moral: don't readily accept any and every engagement hereafter. While you are extremely selective and inflexible in regard to public engagements, someone has only to suggest 'Come to our house,' and you are there the next moment. Move with caution and use your judgement, if you do not want to waste your lifetime hunting up streets where monologous hosts with their loud-voiced wives reside! A valuable day in New York totally destroyed. Suddenly got up in the midst of the other's peroration and said thanks for a lovely evening and good-bye.

Key Obsession

Dinner at the Indian Consulate. The Consul General, a friendly soul without any of the feather and war paint that officials generally love to wear. Other guests for the dinner are an ex-Maharaja from India, whom everyone deliberately 'highnesses' much to his delight. Royalty in exile is generally very exacting. His Highness was a jovial man, with whom I came to backslapping terms before the dinner ended; a morose Muslim officer from the Central Revenue Board, Delhi, who had never heard of me; a Jewish Doctor, before whom everyone was afraid to mention Egypt, but whom everyone asked about 'Tranquility Pills', in order to cover up the Egyptian question which we had been discussing before he arrived. The dinner was a triumph, establishing once for all the supremacy and the tranquilizing qualities of South Indian food—*Rasam, Sambhar, Masala Dosai,* pickles and so forth. I'm more than ever convinced that the South Indian diet marks the peak in the evolution of culinary art and that the South Indian, however well he may be received, will never feel really at home anywhere in the world unless he can have his spices too within reach. My regard for His Highness went up when I found him uttering little cries of joy at the sight of *Sambhar* and *Dosai.* I knew then that the man could do no wrong. It was a commentary on the march of democracy in India that when I mentioned a discount house, where radio sets and refrigerators, could be purchased at a reduced price, His Highness became alert and wanted me to note down the address for him. I did it cheerfully, and also gave a copy of it to our Muslim officer, who brightened up ever so slightly on receiving it and asked what sort of a writer I was and which newspaper I represented. (I had to explain to him gently the distinction between a novel and a newspaper). The good turn I did in providing the address of a discount house so much endeared me to His Highness that he put his arm around my shoulder and cracked a few jokes. He apologized to me in the car when he lit his cigar. All of us compared weights and he envied me for being only 140! He was 196 or thereabouts, but was dieting all the time, which had only the effect of making his suits lose shape ('I have discarded a dozen suits within the last six months!') without any decrease in weight. We went to the United Nations where a debate was in progress in the General Assembly. Mr Menon put us in the V.I.P's gallery, where with the aid of the earphone and push-buttons on your chair you could hear a speech in five languages. It was an impressive setting with a big crowd, colourful furnishing and lights, and a general air of festivity. For a while I diverted myself by listening to a speech in five different languages by pushing the button for a new tongue half way through each sentence, but still I grew bored with it. His Highness was showing me a gold gadget in his vest pocket, which looked like a small pen-knife but was actually a miniature pair of spectacles, with which you could study only a menu card or a list of wines (not at all necessary for one who was reducing). He felt very pleased when I mistook the gadget for a knife, and explained   how he always carried it in his vest-pocket with his latch-key. The word 'Key' made me look for my own room key. It made me anxious when I did not find it in my pocket, and I feared that the stern men at the reception desk of my hotel might refuse to produce a duplicate and leave me to freeze in the open. This thought working at the back of my mind produced an anxiety neurosis in me and completely spoilt for me the United Nations session. I got up abruptly, took leave of His Highness, and rushed back to my hotel, where they gave me a duplicate key without fuss. But when I went up I found that I had not shut the door at all when leaving my room in the morning.

2

THROUGH THE MID-WEST

What Caste, Traveller?

ON the train for Detroit.Very comfortable bed-room suite. Slept soundly. At five-thirty a.m., the steward knocked on my door. Shaved, dressed, and ready at six a.m. Detroit at seven o'clock. I had learnt the art of dealing with porters. I carried two of my bags and left the porter to carry only the other two—so only fifty cents to pay. The porter dumped my bags at a place and told me to await the arrival of 'transfer' man.'Plenty of time, don't worry,' I wondered what was meant by 'transfer'. But one gets used to new phrases and awaits with interest the dawn of their meaning. A new man turned up as promised: 'Lansing, have you got the transfer?' He examined all the papers in my possession, tore off a bit and said, 'O.K. plenty of time. Hang on to your half of the ticket.'

'Grand Rapids?'Get in all passengers for Rapids,'a conductor was shouting and gesticulating on a platform. I said, 'I'm going to East Lansing. Is this the train?' 'Get in, Get in,' he cried impatiently. When I hesitated, he said, 'The train leaves in five minutes, get in.'

I showed him my ticket. He brushed it aside and cried, 'First get in, don't waste time, of course this is your train.' He was excitable like a school boy on his first excursion. I hesitated outside for a moment to enquire about my luggage, but he cried, 'If you don't get in—' gritting his teeth; gesticulating wildly like an air-raid warden ordering the population into the shelter. I could no longer resist this man's unreasonable, irrational, imperiousness. I went in and took a seat. No sign of my luggage. It was a crowded compartment. I asked a passing official, flourishing my ticket, 'Are you sure my seat is here?'

'Ask him,' he pointed at the impatient conductor outside. I was getting worried about my luggage, which a porter had already carried ahead, noting as usual the number of my seat. It was no good hesitating any longer. If my trunks were to be left behind in Detroit, that was just where I was also going to stay. No sense in reaching Lansing to borrow a shirt of the first person I saw. I noticed the hasty conductor already crying 'All aboard', and preparing to lift the steps. I made a quick decision and jumped out, and said, 'My luggage has not come.' He looked at me despairingly as if I were a Peeping Tom, and said,

'The train is about to move—' I lost my temper and cried 'Can't you see that I must have my baggage, what do you mean by hustling me like this? A porter took it from me, where is he?'

Now he showed a better appreciation of my state, 'Let me see your ticket.' When he saw my ticket, his manner changed.

'Oh, your seat is three carriages—further up there; you have a parlour seat reservation, sir.'

'Indeed!' I said, and added, 'And you had no patience to show me my carriage.' He was contrite. Parlour seat belongs to high-caste traveller; and he had subjected me to the indignity of showing me a coach-seat! I had every right to put on the look of a proud soul, deeply hurt. I moved to my parlour car. My suit-cases were there; the attendant said,

'Watch your step, sir,' and 'That is your seat, sir,' 'Let me take your coat'. And, 'Breakfast will be served in a quarter of an hour, sir.' All of which are marks of respectful attention to which a parlour-car passenger is entitled as a birth-right, as opposed to the coach-class one who is generally left alone. Caste system works rigorously in this field. I sat in a swivel chair at the window through which you could watch the landscape gravely.

Steely Thoughts

At the breakfast table a man sitting opposite smiled and said, 'How do you do?'

'Thanks.'

'From India?'

'Yes.' I smiled back affably.

'I am—' he interrupted his breakfast to produce from his pocket a card. It was inscribed: 'Mr So and So, Steel Corporation, Detroit.'

'I am honoured to meet you, sir', I said sufficiently impressed. There was a young man by his side.

'This is my boy who is on a vacation. He goes to school in Chicago. He is Tom.'

I bowed to him too. The man asked,

'Is this your first visit to this country? How do you like it?'

These were routine questions, which I could answer in my sleep. And through the window he pointed out:

'Those are our factories you know.'

'Wonderful, must be . . .' I had no idea how one progressed conversationally with a steel-magnate. To say, 'Must be exciting to produce steel,' or 'You must be making a tremendous lot of money,' might sound silly, so I kept quiet. I looked at Tom appreciatively as he took out a cigarette and lit it. The proud father said,

'We are going to Rapids for a day.' Rapids! It conjured up visions of water-falls cascading over smooth rocks and little glades, the play of sun-light on water producing a hundred rain-bows,—but it was Frank Thomson of Michigan Press, who knocked this vision out by explaining that Rapids was nothing more than another town with its under-car park and market street, not known for anything in particular.

'I am going to East Lansing,' I said.

'Are you connected with the University?' he asked.

'No just visiting.' He now buttonholed me and asked,

'Are you connected with the steel purchasing mission from India?'

'Why?' I asked warily.

'We'd like to sell steel to India, I hear river projects are under way.'

I could now understand his interest in me. I'd shone in borrowed feathers. It was a pity that I should soon be disillusioning him, but I couldn't keep up a steel-talk and was bound to be discovered soon.

So I replied, 'No, I'm not connected with the steel mission.'
'Why?'

I wondered what part of my personality had a steel purchasing touch about it. Then he swung to the other extreme and asked,

'Are you studying in East Lansing?'

'Oh, no, I'm a writer, I mean an author.' It was now his turn to be dumbfounded.

'Must be wonderful to be an author,' or 'Must be making a lot of money,' were probably statements he could not make without feeling silly. So he said, looking at his watch, 'Excuse me, we'll have to be getting back', he smiled, and was off, followed by Tom, puffing away. It made me brood for the rest of my journey how he had come drawn to me like a piece of iron to a magnet, and was repelled the moment he realised I was only an author. For the rest of the journey he hid himself behind his newspaper.

East Lansing

One never expected a mere Lansing to exist in reality—one always thought there could be only East Lansing. At ten-thirty Lansing—a small station. Two men were looking for me. Frank Thomson of the Michigan State University Press, and his Indian friend. From that moment Frank devoted his entire time to me. He drove me in his car to the Kellogg Centre (unforgettable breakfast name) a magnificent hotel, run by students undergoing hotel management course. A very attractive campus—reminded one of Cubbon Park of Ooty.

Pantheon, Parthenon, and Push-Button Ballot

Attended Professor Edward Blackman's lecture on Roman architecture. Forty boys in the class—sat in the last seat of a classroom, after years again. The Professor spoke on Roman viaducts and Ionic columns and pantheon and parthenon, coliseum and so forth. The presence of slaves in ancient Rome made life easy and created a large class of Romans without any occupation. It became necessary to build huge structures and give them continuous free entertainment and enough accommodation to keep the whole population engaged. Some days there were as many as five hundred fights and contests— between men and men, men and animals, and animals and animals—fantastic, and bloody spectacles. The Romans used an enormous quantity of water, '300 gallons per head, that is they consumed each day more water than all the citizens of East Lansing use in a year'. Statistics makes sense only when they are applied to known analogies. I felt impressed. The Romans soon exhausted all the water supply for baths and fountains, and had to devise means of bringing water from distant sources and so built their viaducts.

This was the day of the big election. Impossible to think that one would lecture on a subject like this and anyone would listen to it, while a National Election was in progress. No one seemed to care for it. No holiday. In our country it'd be unthinkable to have schools and offices working on a day like this. Election day ought to be a day of complete, total, abandonment to political excitement.

In my fevered imagination I had expected the election day to be full of noise, crowd and movement, with all normal work suspended; and above all loud-speakers rending the air. Evening a little more activity was noticeable. People were queuing up before the Fire Station; pushed my way through the queue with Frank's help and went in. The polling officials, most of them women, were good enough to explain the working of the mechanical ballot—whereby a push-button records your vote for a party, a member, or a mixture of parties from the President, Supreme Court Judges, down to the Inspector of drains and Municipal Supervisors. Considering the complete overhaul an election involves, surprising that people are not more excited. People went into a curtained booth and recorded their votes. They were silent and business-like. We passed on to another Centre,—a Grammar School where ordinary ballot-paper voting was in progress. Being a grammar school, children were playing in the corridor and moving around with a greater sense of ownership (At the Fire Station too a child had insisted upon being enclosed with her mother in the booth while the officials tried to explain to her how it could not be done). There were fantastic scrawls and figures on the walls. A child held a large Collie by his collar at the door. Four children were watching a garden snake kept in a glass. Women smirked and giggled and commented on political matters. Here again the officials were good enough to explain to me the procedure in voting and the identification of voters was fool-proof.

Kindly Host But–

I must make a mistake in every place and today the mistake was to get tied up with one of my countrymen whom I shall call Joshi. He was a horticulturist, who having married an American, and not knowing where his sympathies lay stopped and debated politics at every corner with all and sundry, to whom in all fairness to myself, I should have said 'No'. I found the horticultural things he took me round to see very limited and uninteresting. I was not interested in watching tropical plants such as banana or coconut raised in glass houses maintained at 70°; while out of my window at home I see nothing but these. We get more horticultural delight in Lal Bagh, Bangalore, or any Mysore nursery. But I'd to pass through several glass houses politely admiring very common, ordinary plants. Like a museum, an official flower garden is a bore. I was tired of the whole thing, but resigned myself to it. I could also sympathise with him—he possessed so much spontaneous friendliness, although he was messy in arranging things. He tried to tie me to a lunch with his office colleagues at eleven in the noon, when he knew full well that I'd had my breakfast only half an hour before. It was painful to say 'no' when his friends wanted me to join them. Joshi had also to put off his own lunch for my sake. Later he took me to the university cafeteria, but forgot that I ate no meat. On the whole confused. I wish I had not put him to the strain of entertainment.

After lunch I was back in my room for an hour. Frank came back to my room and took me to a fat, cheerful, television expert, in an office downstair, where I found Professor Blackman waiting. He was to appear in a television programme along with me. Frank was also in the programme. They both looked very nervous and scared, the television expert kept repeating, 'Television is nothing. Be just natural, don't think of it as something terrible. Forget the boys with their cameras— only just don't do what you were doing now; were you aware that you had your finger across your lips while you spoke just now? It is a thing you simply must not do in a television programme. . . and slightly raise your voice please—not much—but. . .' All of which made Frank so panicky that when he lit his cigarettes in a chain his hands shook, and he confided to me,

'I've never been in this sort of thing before, you know, and I am terrified.'

Financial Expert

After television a visit to Professor Useem's evening class. I was interested to know that my novel *The Financial Expert* had just been studied analytically in that class. I went there dreading how I was going to come through it not remembering much of my own book. It gave me an odd feeling to reflect that a book written in joy and hopefulness in that lonely splendour of my home in Yadavagiri should now be turning up to plague me thus. The class was ready—questions came on to me from various angles: a hand raised, and a question fired at me,

'Is this typical?' 'Is that social tension common?' 'Is that so and so?' 'Do brothers quarrel in India?'

'Of course brothers would quarrel anywhere in the world,' I said and delivered a long discourse on joint-family living in India. About fifty answers, always reminding the audience in conclusion that *The Financial Expert* was a work of fiction, not a treatise or a document, and the story was about an individual and was not portraying a type. 'There are 380 millions in our country, and as many types if you please,' I said, being the only way in which I could explain my point of view.

Ten p.m., applause and close. At the end of the session, one of my audience, an elderly person came up and produced out of his wallet a small group photograph, consisting of about 12 persons—a father, mother, eight sons and two sisters. He explained,

'This is our family, my parents, and brothers. That's me. Till recently we all lived together. It's just to prove to you that some of us also live a joint family life. As long as my parents lived, we were not allowed to leave the old home and live separately. And, that was the happiest period of my life.'

Govind

I have to refer to an Indian friend by a pseudonym because I am making a note about his private life. What happens to an Indian who gets culturally mixed up, was a question that I often put to myself whenever I saw my countrymen abroad. Here in a nutshell this friend provided an answer. I shall call him Govind. He was from an orthodox family in Bombay. He had come to the United States about seven years ago for higher studies. Before he left India, he had been a fervent nationalist, engaged himself in political activities, performed satyagraha, was jailed by the British Government, came under the spell of one of the political leaders of Bombay,—an austere associate of Mahatma Gandhi. This leader is known for his Spartan outlook, a stern practitioner of Gandhian principles of simple living, dedication, and non-killing (for food), and temperance; a man of absolute personal purity in life, and an uncompromising fighter for the principle he feels to be right. Govind came fully under his influence and became his political and personal attache. When he went to the United States for higher studies, Govind was being catapulted into the land of comfort, gadget and beef-steak. He went to school and did well in his studies. He kept in touch with his master, who often wrote to him detailed letters of what was happening in free India, although he was a busy politican. He had real affection for Govind, and promised him that he would personally help him to get suitably settled when he returned to India after his studies. After three years, the young man fell in love with an American (or European, I don't remember) girl, and wrote to his master of his intention to marry her. The master wrote a circumspect letter in reply saying that if Govind felt sure that he was not being carried away by a momentary attraction, he might go ahead. On this blessing the young man married. This was the starting point of complications. His own father, a very orthodox Hindu gentleman, could not view his son's marriage to a European girl with equanimity. He ostracized him from the ancient family. The boy took it calmly, secured a lecturer's post in the University, and settled down with his wife. He had a car, a home, a wife, but still he clung to his orthodox habits and did not eat meat. This created certain domestic complexities and after three years of trial he gave up his orthodoxy, and took to American food. This change of diet seems to have had an unexpected effect on him. For he soon wrote a letter to his master of his conversion. He almost said that he had groped in the dark all along sticking to the precept of his orthodox family and after all light had now dawned. He was now eating meat and was beginning to like it. 'Am actually eating not just ordinary meat, but beef, the best in the world, and it has not done me any harm, it has not destroyed me physically or morally. On the contrary I have never felt better in my life. My point in writing to you about this is this. India will never become a modern nation, unless we Indians get over our blind superstitious prejudice against eating beef. What a shame that we should be begging the world to supply us food? I feel so small when I read in the papers that India is begging for American wheat. We Indians here bow our heads in shame when we read such a piece of news. Instead of it why should we not retain our national self-respect? Beef-eating will solve fifty per cent of our food problem. We allow old cows to stray in public places and remain an economic burden on us; how sensible it would be to slaughter them for food. It will solve our food problem through own effort, and we won't have to be taking around the begging bowl. . . And now this is my point. You must set an example to the nation yourself. You are the first man in our state. If you set an example, others will surely follow you. I would advise you to adopt forthwith beef-eating as a national duty.' This boy had completely lost touch with the realities of an Indian background. Probably suggesting the eating of beef may not sound abnormal in most parts of the world, but in India where the cow is a sacred object, beef cannot be eaten, no rationalization is ever possible on this subject.

The venerable recipient of this advice felt so outraged by the letter, that he wrote a brief reply through his secretary to say that he would prefer not to hear from the young convert again. This episode had its sequel as it made it impossible for Govind to look to his master for support if ever he should return to India.

Govind could stay on in America, but as his wife explained he was gradually becoming home-sick. For about six years he had not thought of his home, his father having cut him off completely. But suddenly his father relented and started sending mementoes every now and then, sweets for *Diwali*, a silk scarf, a brightly-patterned, hand-woven counterpane, and so on. Mrs Govind explained that every time a parcel arrived, Govind would go out of his mind completely. He would parade the gift, and give himself over to sentimental outbursts: 'After all one's parents', 'No place like home', and such things. Govind began to feel that if he wanted to return, his father would certainly receive him and his wife in their ancient home. How this could be practically worked out in an orthodox joint-family, where several others also lived together under the same roof, was a real problem and not a mere matter of detail as our friend had thought. He concluded, 'Well, one of us will always have to be homesick, I suppose, either myself or my wife.' His wife said, 'Don't bother in the least about my homesickness, if you feel sure you want to return home and know what you want to do there.' 'Ah, that is the problem,' he said.

'What am I going to do in India? My master will not help me in the least, and I can't get a foothold anywhere without his help. . . I made a mistake in writing to him that letter. But you see it is only common sense which I wrote, what is wrong in it?' Add to it the fact that they were expecting a baby soon. I will leave him at that, with his 'Buts' and 'However' as unresolved problems.

Self-immolation

The junior member of the staff wanted to 'Buy me a cup of coffee' at the coffee house across the road—a cosy place but smoke-ridden. Talked to them—heaven knows what about. One of the professors of English department came down, joined us and suggested that I should address the Literature students assembled in his class. Walked back to the college. Answered questions about Kipling, Forster, and about myself. On the spot evolved a theory that I started a book on being provoked by an odd and eccentric character. All questions were based on this assumption, and I got plunged more and more in the morass of this hypothesis. Such literary theories are easily enunciated but difficult to maintain unless you hold the monopoly of speech, but the moment one begins to be examined on this issue one is sure to lose ground. I could not maintain my hypothesis too long, finding that my own books would not support the theory. And so when a student asked, 'What about your *English Teacher,* in what way would you call him eccentric or odd?' I was flabbergasted. The boys in their generosity turned to question me on the Passage to India and on Kipling —safe subjects from my point of view.

Last day at East Lansing, packed up in order to 'check-out' at 3 p.m. Met the famous American artist Rattner and Mrs Rattner at the Cafeteria for a few minutes and got involved in a discussion about the need for prayer and meditation in daily life (particularly for Americans). Saw some of his pictures and felt baffled by his style but felt too polite to say so; he looks so venerable.

*

At noon, over lunch, faced an interview by a press reporter. He had had an appointment to meet me at breakfast, but actually turned up during lunch at the restaurant table, explaining that he had been called away by a sudden scoop about a triple murder. I wanted to know all about it, but he would not say anything more. He treated it casually —I'm afraid with a deliberately put-up professional air of boredom and casualness. He looked fatigued and bored—from three corpses to a live Indian author was all in his day's range of work, undoubtedly. I could not get over the feeling that he was not a real reporter (Just as I could not help the feeling that the Kellogg Centre with its perfect service was a make-believe place), but a type out of the pages of a whodunit—the sort of reporter who beats both the detective and sergeant at their game of investigation. Over the soup he asked, 'What solution would you offer for the American civilization? What can save it?'

'What is wrong?'

'We have everything in the world, yet are unhappy. We as a nation are terribly bored; and so seek continuous forgetfulness in excitement, gadgets and so forth. Our suicide rate is increasing, our divorce rate doubling. What do you think it's due to? What solution would you suggest?'

'Meditation and withdrawal—for about fifteen minutes a day,' I said echoing the talk with Rattner in the morning.'In every Indian home we have a place called the *Puja* room or God's room, where the members of a family could generally withdraw and pray. Most Indians pray and meditate for at least a few minutes every day, and it may be one of the reasons why, with all our poverty and struggle, we still survive, and are able to take a calm view of existence. I cannot say that we have appreciable suicide-rate in our country; practically no divorce.'

'Do you attribute it to the presence of the special room in every Indian home? What do you call it?'

'*Puja,* Puja in Sanskrit means worship'

'Will you please spell it for me?'

He fishes out of his pocket a crumpled piece of paper of almost the size of a bus ticket, from amidst his handkerchief, cigarettee-packet etc., smooths its out, and jots down in a corner the word 'Puja', and stuffs it away back into the folds of his kerchief and matches. He then goes on to enquire about the literary trends in modern India, and of course I have to mention our epics, and so he has to retrieve the bus ticket again and again to note down names. If ever anyone has an occasion to take a look at that bit of paper he will find on it 'Ramayana', 'Mahabharatha', 'Tagore', 'Gandhi', 'Sathyagraha', 'Nehru', 'Tamil', 'Telugu', 'Sanskrit', etc. I don't know if he had the patience or the space to write down all the names I kept mentioning as I found him attempting to make a note, jotting a vowel or a consonant, and abandoning it immediately. I speculated how he would weave all this jumble into a copy.

Perhaps on the other side of the bus ticket was the sketch of triple murder. Would both get a page-wide splash in whatever the paper he was representing?   Is it possible *The Three in One Homicide* juxtaposed with *Indian Author Recommends Quarter Hour Meditation for Would-be Suicides* or *Puja Room Abolishes Divorce in India.* I had all along thought that he was there as my guest but he suddenly called for his check, paid for his portion of the lunch, and was off, and I had no chance of asking what he proposed to do with all that jumble of names on his bus ticket.

On to Madison

The train from Chicago to Madison is not a very serious train. It reminds one of Nizam's State Railways of old days. I held a first-class ticket but no one would let me into a 'Parlour car' because all the seats had been reserved for a 'Football' crowd.

'Are you going to the ball game?' the guard kept asking.

'No,' I said.

'Then, you must go up, we can't take you here.'

I had to walk the entire length of the enormous train and then they put me into a crowded 'coach' which is, as I have already said, parallel to our third class. No one cared to understand what I said as I kept repeating that I held a first-class ticket.

The train strolled along at its own pace—an unpunctuality which no one would have dared to attempt in our country (at least in olden times). It stopped and switched off the engine at various stations, a big noisy football crowd streamed in all along the way and choked all the space, crying 'Scandalous arrangements!'Football was too much in the air. Everyone asked of everyone else something about North-Western and Wisconsin. This was a bad day for normal travellers—the Saturday afternoon train. I was again and again asked by ticket-checking officials whether I was going to the match.

'No, no, no.'

'Then you will have to move up to the other coach, this is stopping at the football ground.'

I am a heretic in this land of football worshippers. In other days they might have burned me at the stake. With all this diversion the train arrived at Madison late beyond count, and when I was hoping to leave the train once for all, it stopped within sight of the station, a furlong away and spent another half an hour detaching the coaches occupied by the football patrons.

Henry Hart, whom I'd known intimately at Mysore, and his little daughter Nancy, are there to receive me. When I finally manage to find my way out of the carriage. This is another penalty that a 'coach' traveller has to pay—he'll have to wait till everyone ahead has cleared out of the carriage. Talk of class-distinctions! Remember I'd a first class ticket all the time in my pocket! I'm entitled to a refund, I think, but no one will explain to me the procedure for claiming it.

Adam Street

Henry and Virginia give me a room in their lovely home in Adam Street. It was Nancy's room till a moment ago; for her toys peep at me from their various corners of concealment. I feel completely at home. Henry, Virginia, Benny, and Nancy, and their huge shaggy dog Tippy (mixed Collie and Airedale), form a happy household; with another Virginia, a bright girl in a green dress who appears at the dining table and vanishes unobtrusively into her own room upstairs. She is a student who has room and board here in return for helping Virginia with household and baby-sitting a couple of days in the week when Virginia goes out of town to teach. Within a couple of hours of my arrival, I am involved in parties. Cocktails somewhere, and then on to a dinner at a French Professor's house, where through Virginia's gentle hints I am provided with a plate of rice and vegetables. A young man who has just won a seat in a local election and his wife, a well-read tiny French girl seem to be the guests of honour today, and the talk is all about the elections at Milwaukee and the machinations of the opposite camp. The young man never speaks a word for hours, until someone starts him on the subject of elections, and then he reels off all the stories of individuals, groups, unions, up-town or down-town associations, which attempted to wreck his chance. He doesn't seem to have got over the surprise of getting through the election successfully. He speaks in a sort of monotonous iambic meter, moving no part of his face except his jaws, his wife collaborating in the narrative in a sort of undertone running commentary. I feel completely lost. The French host's friendliness and cheerfulness are stimulating, but alas, he speaks so little. He just smiles and serves food and drink, while the budding Milwaukee politician and his wife do all the talking— the rest are just so many pairs of ears for them. Before leaving I say to the Milwaukee monologist, 'Hope you will end up in Washington someday,' at which his face relaxes. Rather a handsome gesture on my part since neither he nor his talkative wife ever bother to ask who I am, or how I have come to find myself in their midst.

A Bright Sunday

Sunday morning. The day is bright when I wake up at nine o'clock. Find the family ready for breakfast. A sunny and promising day. It stimulates people to make plans and announce them.

Henry says, 'I am going to get into old clothes and fix Benny's cart.' This is a dog cart, a two wheeled trap to which the hefty Tippy is yoked and driven about by Nancy or Benny, flourishing a whip. A nice contraption which may be seen in front of Henry's house at Adam's Street any time of the day or night. But Henry is a perfectionist who likes to work on the sled again and again. He has a complete workshop at the basement, and his idea of relaxation is to fix things at his workshop. He disappears after this announcement. I say, catching the mood of the hour,

'I will go for a walk,' the only way in which I can enjoy a bright day.

Virginia says, 'There is a park nearby with a zoo, let's all go there with the children.' The children receive the proposal with a whoop of joy. I go up-stairs to dress. Benny, Nancy, and Tippy go after Henry. I come down an hour later, dressed and ready to go out. Virginia is washing dishes.

'We will go after this,' she says to me.

Henry comes in unobtrusively and lends a hand in washing.

Over the splash of the faucet Virginia suddenly asks,
  'Where is Benny?'
  'I managed to fix his carriage, now it nicely fits on Tippy. They are there—playing.'
  'Have you left Benny alone with the dog?'
  'Nancy is also there.' Silence. Over the sound of flowing water Virginia says quietly,
  'They should not be left alone by themselves, Henry.'
  'Why not?'
  'Oh, I don't know they may run away. Why have you left them there?'
  'I came to help you wash.'
  'No, I don't like it Henry.'
  'I will go back to them presently.'
  'Leave me to do the washing. Please go.'
  'I insist upon helping you', says Henry jocularly. The humour is lost on her.
  Virginia says in deadly seriousness, 'I don't think you should leave them alone, Henry.'
  'Nancy is with them,' says Henry.
  I notice the same set of arguments coming up in a second cycle while the faucet splashes, their talk is being carried on in the gentlest undertone but gradually gathers emphasis. I feel that my presence embarrasses them and that they might perhaps have it out a little more decisively if I left them free. I quietly withdraw from the scene and go back to my room and settle down to do a little writing. I write my diary notes of four days, having been in arrears, and I am occupied thus for an hour. When I finish writing I strain my ears to hear their voices and to guess what stage of the debate they may be in now. There is dead silence below. I concluded that peace must have again settled on the household and that Henry must have gone back to guard the children. I put away my papers and go downstairs. Virginia is cleaning up the gas stove with a sort of grim determination. I wonder if she will be free now to come out into a bright day with me. She hears my footsteps. As I pause at the door she says quietly, 'Benny is lost.' She adds, 'I knew something would happen. Henry has gone to search for him.'

'What about Nancy? Wasn't she with him?'

'I don't know,' she says without lifting her head. She is probably in tears. Benny had been seated in the sled carriage with Tippy yoked to it at the time Henry had come in offering to do dish-washing. Nancy who was supposed to be with them was hailed by a friend and moved away absentmindedly, leaving Benny alone. By the time they were all back to look for him, Virginia's premonition had been fulfilled. Virginia looks so unhappy that I cannot help asking,

'Why are you so worried?'

'He is so small, anything may happen to him, with so many cars about. . .'

I suddenly feel that I ought to join in the search for Benny. I go out.

At the end of the street I see Henry leading Tippy, who is of course, strapped to his carriage, but without Benny in his seat, 'I caught Tippy running down Randal. Benny and Nancy must have got off together somewhere,'says Henry, the optimist he is.

'So it is o.k., they should both be back soon.'

But this is a false lull. Presently Nancy comes running down the road from another direction.

'Where is Benny?'

'I didn't see him,' she says innocently baring her gums. 'They were here,' she says assertively indicating the spot where she last saw them. She catches hold of Tippy by his shaggy ears and shouts,

'Tippy, where is Benny? Where is Benny?' Tippy merely sweeps his huge fan-like tail, pants, and puts his tongue out. Henry bends close to Tippy and says,

'Tippy my man, look, you have really tipped Benny over somewhere. Where is he?' Tippy shakes his entire gawky frame, rolls his eyes, and lets out a bark in joy at being addressed, and tries to stand on his legs and jump although hindered by the harness and reins of the sled; giving almost a demonstration of what he could do with a rider sitting in the carriage. All of us stand looking helplessly at the animal wishing that he could speak.

Nancy says, 'I will go and look for him.'

'No Nancy go back home, I don't want to search for you next,' but Nancy begs,

'Daddy, I won't get lost. Let me look for Benny please,' it is evident that she enjoys the thrill of this search;and will not miss it for anything. She runs down the road again out of sight. Henry now looks serious. He goes up the steps and peeps in at the kitchen door just to report to Virginia, 'Not found yet,' and goes out again, on his bicycle this time. Virginia sits unmoved in the kitchen chair and murmurs, 'Something terrible must have happened to him. He is so small. He can't even speak. I don't know. . . Probably he has been kidnapped. That sort of thing is common here. I don't know if I shall ever see him again.' I say inanely, 'He couldn't have gone far'. 'What is he wearing?' I ask.

'A brown jumper and green cap. I must telephone the police.'

'Oh, no, don't,' I say, somehow not liking the idea of police being involved in it.

'He has probably been kidnapped, such things are common here.'

I go out in search of Benny. Though Madison is not a very big town, when it comes to searching for someone its streets look endless and complicated. I walk up and down and across the streets and go back and forth, looking for a brown jumper and green cap. To me every child looks like Benny. Benny is chubby, round-headed, and pink, about a foot and a half high; that is all the impression I have of him, nothing more detailed. Being a sunny Sunday scores of Benny-like children are moving around and most of them seem to wear green caps. I stare so much at every child I pass that they start running at the sight of me. I block the passage of one or two to say 'Hallo!' and ask,

'Where are you going?'

'I am going home.'

'Where do you live?'

My questions have the effect of making them run back to their houses. So I watch every child get back to his house, rather a complicated process of eliminating non-Benny's. I believe I am scaring all the children off the streets this morning, as I go about with that fixed examining look. I notice here and there at a cross-road Henry pedalling his cycle slowly with his eyes on the passing children. About an hour later, I notice a van slowly perambulating with policemen peeping out of it, obviously looking for a green cap. The children of the town must be having a puzzling morning with everyone staring at them so purposefully.

I give up the search after about two hours. I go to a milk bar for a drink and start homeward to report failure. Virginia has laid the table for lunch and is waiting for me. Benny is back. I find him engrossed in his lunch, perched on his high chair. He must be ravenously hungry after his outing and cannot wait for others. Virginia is her usual cheerful self again.

'Did the police pick him up?' I ask.

'No. They had come to say that they could not find him and wanted to alert the neighbourhood. When they went back to their car, they found Benny examining it; and then they picked him up and brought him in; actually, you know, no one found Benny. He found himself.'

'Where did you go Benny?' I ask.

He pauses with the soup wet around his mouth, smacking his lips,

'There,' he says pointing from his seat of eminence, indicating a far-away beyond.

'Where?' I cannot help asking out of curiosity.

He merely replies, 'Walk,' and with that monosyllable returns to his lunch, dismissing the affair once and for all from his thoughts, having successfully neutralized all our elaborate plans for a bright Sunday morning.

Speech-Correction

In the evening visit the University Union to hear Katherine Ann Porter read her short stories. Very unimpressive show. Her masterpiece 'At the Circus' which is so good to read sounds feeble and pointless at her reading. Moral: an author should never give a reading of his or her own masterpiece, nor should he try to explain it. It always produces an effect of bathos. The hall is full. To think that people have bought tickets for this. Extraordinary habits. In our own country, the way to assure an empty hall would be to announce a price for seats at the lecture. On the contrary, speakers being so much more eager than their audience, they may have to tempt them with gifts in order to fill the seats. But this is a land where anyone would gladly give a dollar or two for sitting through an hour's lecture.

Rest of the evening at the Union Cafe—smoke filled, beer-flowing. Students were dispersed here and there; some were writing their assignments. This was the only student organization where beer was served because as some one explained there was a large body of Germans here, and also because the Milwaukee breweries were nearby and had something to do with the universities. Noisy music. We sat chatting at the top of our voices sipping our drinks.

Conversational atmosphere rather spoilt by one of the ladies, Mrs R—, who caught me telling Virginia, 'Gill suddenly developed pneumonia,' and would not let me proceed, her amusement at the way I said *develop* was so great. 'All Indians say *develop, committee;* instead of De-Vellop, and 'Committee'—'Does *Pneumonia* develop?' she said, which I found very irritating. I merely replied, 'So much of accent seems to me a waste of good breath; we've always been taught to speak without accent. Do you imagine your way of accenting is the most desirable, which the whole world should copy? In any case, why don't you let me finish my sentence so that you may catch the sense of what I am trying to say.' I could not speak more rudely since she was cheerful and nice otherwise, and had left her car at our disposal the whole day. She was not to be curbed so easily. The whole evening she kept repeating 'So Pneumonia developed! H'm!' and enjoyed the joke afresh each time although the rest of the company could not share her humour and wanted to talk of other things. Before bidding goodnight she again concluded, 'What did you say, "Pneumonia developed", is it?' and giggled.

I had a premonition that this preoccupation with Pneumonia would do her no good. My premonition was confirmed when I received an unsigned postcard two days later with the message:

'The pity would be
If by accident or design
Your present accent ever stopped
Accept an admirers wishes
That you continue to say
Your friend's Pneumonia *Developed.*'

On the day I left Madison, I telephoned to this lady intending to say good-bye; but I could not reach her as she was indisposed and could not be disturbed. A month later Virginia wrote to me, while giving me local news, 'Mrs R—was down with severe double Pneumonia. I am happy to say that she is out of danger, but still the doctor says she will have to be very careful for some months.' I could only wish that she would not invite a relapse by recollecting me and attempting a fresh set of verse on Pneumonia.

Space and Time

The problem of parking is one that lends a touch of irony to the whole development of modern transport. Every third person has a car, which means every third man needs a space of 22 by 5, wherever he goes. Everywhere one turns one notices the warning: 'Parking between. . .' 'Reserved for. . .' 'Absolutely no parking'. 'No parking at any time', places where one must jump out of a moving car in order to reach one's destination. The problem is to get to a place in a car and get off at the right spot, otherwise you might as well walk from the starting point itself. There are parking facilities only for twelve minutes duration or for ten hours. You slip the appropriate coin into the meter and return in time to take out the car, otherwise the inexorable dial betrays you to the police and brings you a ticket tucked behind the windscreen wiper—a long envelope at the sight of which the driver knows that he will have to part with several dollars on the following day. It means you will have to be watching your watch, which incidentally seems to support the sale of watches. Parking in certain places is permitted for higher officials and a junior who demands it will not get it: there is a local tale of an indignant junior, who resigned his job, stood for elections, became a senator and parked his car at the best place in the same compound within a year. There are radar beams which betray the speed and cameras which photograph the number plate of the offending motor car, there are young men who hold up placards to say 'Radar-check beware' in order to confound the police trap.

Live Lobster

At twelve p.m., Henry took me along to meet Miss. . ., someone or the other, name has gone out of my mind, Chairman of the English Department, who was all excited about a conference she was attending at Washington. Lunched with her and three others of the English Department. As usual with the English department anywhere, they were cautious and on the defensive. They may not have heard of me or read my books, quite understandably, but they were in a suspense lest I should shoot questions at them. I for one do not in the least mind if others don't read me. They are not bound to. I don't read the books they write. So it is all right with me. But what I do object to is their defensiveness in my presence. They seem to be all the time in a suspense lest I should put questions to them on my work. 'Compare my *Financial Expert* with *Swami and Friends,*' 'What is the English title of *Grateful to Life and Death?*' *'When was Mahatma published?'* and so on. I am a very considerate author, never referring to my work unless I am forced to. At this lunch, my neutral attitude proved encouraging, because in a short while conversation began to flow. My hosts ventured to ask,

'How many languages are there in India?'

'Fourteen.'

'So many. Are books being written in all of them?' 'What are the literary trends most noticeable? After Independence, has Indian writing shown any notable change? etc., etc., . . .?'

And then they came near to the most dangerous question,

'Are your books translated?'

'Into what?'

'English?'

'I write in English.' This brought the conversation on to the edge of the precipice. Fortunately we had got through the desserts by then and everybody looked at his watch, and planned his retreat, saying,

'I've a class.'

'Oh, I have a meeting,' or

'I'm flying for a conference in Washington. I must catch the plane. . .' English studies work on the basis that a dead author is a good author. He is passive and still while you explain and analyse him in the class-room; having a living author on hand may be like having a live lobster on your plate.

Wrightism

One of Henry's friends interested in architecture, brings his car in order to take me through the town and show Frank Lloyd Wright's designs and Sullivan's before him—fantastic houses with horizontal lines at all costs. Frank Lloyd Wright's deliberate *negligé* [leaving portions of a building rugged without plaster or dressing] seems to us rather affected, but one must see them through the eyes of Americans who are probably sick of machine-finish everywhere, and who may have a fascination for the half-finished look. To me such an ultra-modern building appears like the house of a man, in our country, who has run out of cash and cannot induce his contractor to plaster the walls. Americans cherish antiquities—in many of the homes, the most cherished object is a piece of mat or a brass vase or a verdigris-covered image from India, while in an Indian home the proudest possession would be a chromium-finished cigarette-lighter or a cuckoo-clock from Switzerland, one half of the world always yearns for something that the other half possesses but does not care for. In New York, in some of the more fashionable restaurants, an extra attraction is provided by the announcement, 'Charcoal broiled steak', and behind the glass, the roasting being done in public view, with firewood burning in brick kilns with real smoke going up, similar to the open-air kitchens built in preparation for a large-scale marriage feast in any household in an Indian village.

*

Returned home and went out for a walk; Nancy insisted upon keeping me company (riding) in her dog-cart. This proved a too complicated companionship. She was in her sled drawn by Tippy and me on the road, the dog sometime racing up, sometimes at a standstill or sometimes prancing like a pony. So pursuaded her to go back home and leave me alone. After a walk returned in time for an Indian dinner, of rice and curry devised by Virginia; a number of Professors and their wives were invited. After dinner shut the doors and built a fire with all the guests sitting around—really cheerful and cosy, the temperature outside being very low. The fire was built as usual with the Sunday issue of the *New York Times* (which Henry maintains is excellent, adequate fuel). The children were sent to bed early. If they were around, lighting a fire became an elaborate ritual—the children being ever ready to feed the fire with varied literary fare. Henry had only to announce, 'Let us build a fire,' and Nancy and Benny would gather all the magazines, books, letters, and manuscripts they could lay hands on and dump them in the fire-place. While Henry always thought this an excellent disposal of much of his correspondence and unwanted library stock, Virginia sometimes complained that some of her letters were thus destroyed even before she got a chance to see them. The climax was reached one day when Benny tore sheets out of a brand-new copy of Oxford World Atlas for feeding the fire. He was punished for it (as at times when he bit Nancy) by being carried to his bed; his protests on such occasions took the form of blood-curdling cries and shouts from behind the door, and then he'd kick against the door (to which Tippy would respond by barking merrily and scratching the door with his claws from this side), until sleep overcame him, the rest of the family going about their business unmindful of the uproar.

*

When Nancy peeped in at my door, I asked, from my bed what the time was. She promptly said 'Eight' and withdrew her head. Continued to sleep, for half an hour more, believing her; but found that it was nearly eleven when I got up and had my first coffee. Skipped breakfast and went up to pack. Packed and ready to leave at three.

No Time for Good-bye

The train is at five p.m. At four-thirty we are all out in the street looking for a wireless-summoned-taxi. I cannot say good-bye to Nancy as she is away somewhere else playing or watching television. Benny is coming with us to the railway station. He is excited at the prospect of seeing a train, asking a hundred questions, employing over and over again the limited vocabulary at his disposal and trying to squeeze the maximum sense into them. At the station the official behind the window says, after taking a look at my ticket,

'No Parlour seat in the five o'clock train, only coach class.'

'But you sold us a first class ticket yesterday!'

'Oh, that was a mistake. You can travel coach and claim a refund later.'

I feel that for the next few months I shall have no time for anything but writing claims for refund of tickets sold by mistake. When the train steams in, Henry like a good host, will not let me touch a bag but carries all the five pieces himself, into a coach, hauling them up, and moving them to a corner.

And now a train official comes up to look at my ticket and exclaims,

'You have a first class ticket, you must go further up.'

'But they said there is no first class on this train!'

'Who? The office staff there, they wouldn't know.' None seems to know of any matter precisely. I refuse to move again, preferring to continue where I have found myself. But they won't hear of it. Never heard of a coach class being occupied by a parlour car traveller (although this was exactly what had happened to me while coming to Madison on that day of the football match). So once again we are on the move. Only a few seconds left. The ticket has once again to be taken to the office for revised payments and checking and so on, Henry runs to the other end of the platform for endorsing a reservation. I pick up my baggage and get a porter to move my baggage to my legitimate seat in the parlour compartment, where a set of grim, determined patricians are elegantly leaning back in their swivel chairs reading their papers pausing ever so slightly to watch the last minute arrival into this exclusive paradise. Virginia and

Benny are waiting to have a few words before I leave. It is so difficult to squeeze in a word in all this confusion and last minute make-shift. Benny does not care, his gaze being rivetted on the engine of which he has now a near-view. I hardly have the time to thank Virginia for all her kindness, the train is about to leave, Henry comes running with the new reservation tickets. There is just enough time to snatch the ticket from his hand and jump into my compartment .before the steps are removed. All through the journey I am racked with the thought that I ought to have managed to spend a little more time talking to Virginia and Henry instead of letting my luggage monopolize my attention.

3

CHICAGO

In Professors' Midst

BETWEEN Singer, Redfield,* and Shils, eminent Professors whose knowledge of India was profound and who had each spent at least a year in different parts of India, my stay in Chicago was most rewarding. Between them they unobtrusively took care of my food, shelter, and movements.

On the morning of my arrival while talking to Redfield in his room, Milton Singer came in to say that Chamu was arriving from New York next day. Let no one be puzzled about the identity of Chamu. He is Dr M. N. Srinivas, an eminent Indian sociologist of Oxford, Baroda, Bombay, Manchester and Delhi, who was a great friend and neighbour of mine in Mysore. Years ago when I wrote my first novel *Swami and Friends,* and found none to read it, a very young college fellow came forward to go through the manuscript; he read and certified it as readable, which was very encouraging. That was Chamu. He was then a college student; now he is a senior, respected professor—many academic activities and distinctions having come his way. His research and studies constantly took him out of view, if not to another corner of the world at least to another part of the country. However I always had an annual glimpse of him, when he came down for a couple of weeks each year to see his mother and brothers in Mysore. Our literary contact started years ago with *Swami* continued. He always goaded me on to write my

* Alas now dead.

next and not to waste my time; whenever I saw him I discussed with him the subject I had in mind for a new novel, and through his reaction I always got an objective view of anything I might plan to write. So he continued, through years, to be not only the first reader of my first book, but also a critic and adviser on many unwritten ones.

Now I was happy to know that I should be seeing him next day, not only because I longed to speak Tamil to someone but I also hoped he would be able to give me a small quantity of betel-nut to which I am addicted. I had exhausted my own stock of it weeks ago; above all I wanted to speak to him about my new book and the problems connected with it.

I stayed at the Quandrangle Club, a residential club for Faculty members and their guests. I had a comfortable room upstairs and everything was fine. After breakfast Professor Shils called on me and took me along to the college. Afternoon Milton Singer suggested that I might attend a class (or was it a seminar, I can never say, the only difference between the two being that in a seminar the students light their cigarettes during the lecture but in a class probably they don't. Here I found in Cohn's classroom everyone smoking). Milton Singer and I sat at one end of a horse-shoe table.

The lecture is on Indian Joint-Family. Joint-Family is almost a rage in academic circles in this country. Whenever I go questions are fired at me on joint-family, their real wonder being how so many different persons could live, work, and budget-balance, under the same roof. I have always stressed the point about the joint family that this system of living affords protection to the oldest and the youngest in a family. A family in which several brothers live together with their wives and children produces an extreme sense of security in the children, who move with all the members of the family freely, and when their parents go out there is no problem of engaging a baby-sitter; the children do not feel lonely, as they generally spend their time with their cousins, uncles or grandparents. As a matter of fact, in a big household children hardly ever cling to their parents. They get a balanced training as they are always watched by someone or the other and if they are spoilt by their parents they get certainly disciplined by uncles or others and *vice versa*. Anyway children grow up very well in a corporate household, without neurosis, angularities, or over-sensitiveness. For old people their original domestic life has an appearance of continuance, the old parents never lose touch with the affairs of the family, giving plenty of advice and guidance, sometimes offering even a different point of view, all of which gives them a feeling of having something to do.

Cohn has drawn an elaborate chart of a joint-family with a lot of sociological jargon thrown in, he has also drawn a chart of the interior of a large village home to show how members are dispersed in a large household. It is interesting to watch all this, and the variety of questions asked by the boys on this complicated arrangement. It is very interesting to view myself as a specimen of this system. At the end of his lecture I am asked questions on my book *The Bachelor of Arts* which has been just studied in the class as an example of Indian life. The boys fire away questions at me and once again I am at a disadvantage, having read and written so much else after *The Bachelor of Arts*. As usual they ask, 'Is that scene on page such and such typical of an Indian family household? Could Chandran's life be considered an example of a joint-family living?' and so on.

The Chair

Yesterday Lyle Blair's long distance call from East Lansing woke me to say that he was coming to see me today. Early this morning phone-call again from him to say that he will not come as the plane flights have been cancelled owing to bad weather. Dark, dismal day with a cold wind blowing. After breakfast ventured out for a walk. Saw a barber's shop on the way and walked in, with a slight misgiving as I remembered the following story told by Balaraman of New York. An Indian artist on a travel assignment from India happened to be in Chicago and went to a barber's shop for a hair-cut. The barber refused to admit him owing to his colour. The man was so demoralized by it that he returned to New York and shut himself in his room not having the confidence to show himself outside again. Balaraman had to visit him each day and pursuade him to venture out as he feared that the artist was going to starve and die in his room,—ultimately the man had to cancel all his plans for a study-tour and return home. But this Chicago barber welcomed me. 'Saloon' same as ours, only the pictures hanging on the wall were less garish. The barber wore a snow-white apron and blue trousers, and ran an electric-clipper over one's scalp. He turned the chair away from the mirror while cutting the hair—sensible arrangement as it saved the contemplation for a prolonged period of one's head in a composite frame with the barber's. When he felt that you were entitled to have a glimpse of yourself in the mirror, he flicked the seat around asking: 'Is it all right?' Before you might study yourself too well, he turned it away again. After a few slight touches with scissors he held a hand mirror for a second, too close to your eyes, and you saw yourself blurred.

'Awful weather, isn't it?' I said to make conversation.

He shook his head, 'The temperature is going down if anything, too cold—it ought not to be so at this time of the year, surely.'

'I'd my last hair-cut in Bombay', I said to impress him.

'That was a long way back for a hair-cut, sir,' he said. He was interested to know that I would be going to California.

'You are going to a fine place, let me tell you', he said. As usual in all strata of society, California spells magic. Meanwhile the other barber who had been listening to the radio, said,

'Fifty thousand persons to have Thanksgiving Dinner—with turkey and everything. Who pays for it? The tax-payer,' he said with a profound, disturbing civic conscience. He explained to me how and why these things happened, and what and who were at the back of all that show. After the hair-cut was over, a little flick off here and there, and a run of the comb on the hair (no lotion and dressing as in our country, unless perhaps you asked for it). When I got up, my barber went to the cash machine and said without facing me, 'That'd be two dollars twenty, today, sir; . . . because,' he felt a little apologetic, 'it's Thanksgiving tomorrow.' Everything was now hitched to Thanksgiving. Ahead, back, and on the day itself, Thanksgiving Day seemed to loom large. The charges as printed on the wall were only 1.75. He raised it by 25 cents and added another twenty to it. I paid down with a look of casual ease and cheerfulness, without any betrayal of shock, feeling that my barber in India would not earn it from me for a whole year's attention to my head.

Visited the Museum, and started back for my room. The barber waved to me from his seat when I passed his shop again. Evidently the extra forty-five cents had cemented a friendship between us.

*

Night dinner with Shils. I am moved by his solicitous hospitality. He prepares my dinner with his own hand; he lays the table, serves, changes plates, and is constantly moving in and out. He is a complete host. I protest against the extraordinary trouble he is taking but he brushes aside my protest. 'I enjoy doing this for you,' he says.

After dinner adjourn to his study where books cover the walls and rise to the ceiling. He is a man of varied studies, knowledge and incisive observations—it is engrossing to hear him talk: personalities, politics, and books.

As we sit there lost in conversation, we hear the thud of a falling object in the next room, followed by a scream. Find that his child has rolled off his bed in sleep and fallen down. I feel unhappy. Perhaps I am indirectly responsible for this mishap: normally perhaps Shils and his wife would have retired with the child and prevented its fall. Shils looks anxious, still makes an effort not to leave a guest alone. I take my leave, being the only thing I could do to help him. He is good enough to say: 'Don't go, he'll be all right,' though his face is full of anxiety. While giving me my coat, he notices that it is light. He fetches his own, heavy coat and wraps it around my shoulder, remarking, 'Should you catch a cold, of all places, in Chicago?' and sees me off. Later I was relieved to learn that the child continued his sleep unmindful of the fall and woke up quite normally in the morning.

*

Thanksgiving day. Awakened by the telephone call from the

manager's desk.

'Breakfast being served, sir, and will close in a few minutes. If you are coming down I can tell them to wait for ten minutes.'

'Thanks, time please?. . . .'

'Nine-twenty. . . .'

'I'll come down in a second.' I jump out of my bed, hurriedly wash and dress up, and go down to breakfast. Thanksgiving drives everyone away, and depletes the town of all its useful men and women.

Chandran of U.S.

I know that all the restaurants close today at seven. But still attempt to go out to try my luck, protected with ear-muffs (which always makes me feel silly) and Shil's great coat, dreading the cold outside. But the young man at the desk comes to my rescue. He opens the store, brings me a tray of food to my room although he confesses that he is not sure if he has authority to open the store. However it saves me from starvation or the alternative of searching for an open restaurant and getting frozen in the process.

After dinner go down for a chat with the young man. His name is Montague something. He feels Montague rather Shakespearean and unlucky in romance. His girl is in California. They love each other but still have not decided whether they should marry. He is preparing for a diploma in 'Fine Arts' but also works part-time at the hotel desk. Hopes ultimately to make enough money to take a trip to California. He has not decided what he should do for a career—he alternates between various proposals and possibilities; he is the American version of Chandran of my *Bachelor of Arts*. He is thrilled to hear that I shall be visiting at Palo Alto—where his sweetheart is studying.

'I don't know, I don't know, what we are waiting for,' he says. He adds, 'After I marry, I shall also become a vegetarian like you, because I think it'll save us a lot of money. You look O.K. without eating meat. Why should I also not try? In any case, after I'm married, I may not afford to pay for meat. Another thing—I once saw a chicken killed in our kitchen and never got over the shock. I have no right to eat something which

I can't see killed.'

On Thanksgiving 70 (or 700) million turkeys are consumed in the state—on this day the general paralysis of public life is thorough—no letters delivered at all! No shop, no bank, nothing doing, 'no, nothing' (to quote a Los Angeles downtown hotel clerk). This is a 'Legal' holiday, which means it is a complete one. Friday, that's tomorrow is going to be a holiday without much legal mention, I'm sure, because it's wedged in between Saturday and today.

At the Zoo

S—, who teaches in the University, with his brother and all the members of the family, called at my hotel at 10 a.m. in order to take me to the zoo. It was a very considerate act on his part, considering the fact that the car was full of the members of his family who had come for Thanksgiving. He took me to the zoo, stopping at the Chicago Bank for my sake, where I sent off a remittance home. We drove through the snow: glorious white everywhere. Driving was difficult. At the zoo it was impossible for me to move about—the temperature was probably 20° all through and the cold was intense; my toes were numb under the shoe, my nose felt like a wood-chip, losing its sensitivity. Everyone expected with a lot of thrill tonight's temperature to go down to 5°! The zoo was very much like other zoos, with miserable animals in heated chambers—the monkeys, elephants and tigers seemed resigned like those under a life sentence. I was impressed with the gorillas I saw. S— had a habit like zoo visitors all the world over, of making animal noises on his side of the cage, and disturbing the dignity of all those reposeful animals. At the conservatory their wonderment at the sight of mostly yellow chrysanthemums surprised me. Lunched with them at a restaurant across the road on spaghetti and tomato. Very soon I got tired of the zoo, and felt convinced that I had messed up another day. On the way back Mrs S— insisted upon being driven through a certain road and in front of some houses, where she had spent her childhood. She became very sentimental in this district and narrated anecdotes of how she used to go up such and such a distance which seemed so big then. At the zoo also, earlier in the day she had been, excitedly pointing at various objects, a Viking ship, (1,000 A.D.) which she used to admire as a child, a water fountain where she used to stand on a slab of stone to reach the spout. 'Oh, how high up it seemed to be then!' all of which was appreciated and approved with screaming giggles by S—'s sister. I fear that gentle S— found all this reminiscencing a little tedious and embarrassing. Reminiscencing might not always be a suitable occupation, it should be something personal like one's bank balance. It may not thrill everyone to see a house where one was born or bred, unless the person happened to be a Shakespeare or Keats. There were other fallacies too in this attitude: Mrs S— was not really removed far enough to reminisce and feel sentimental either in time or space. She was recollecting something that happened less than five and not seventy years ago. And the place was only a couple of miles from where she now lived: someone even asked why she didn't think of coming up here all these days to indulge in reminiscences, instead of waiting for our company. I realized soon that I was no longer fit for company, and when S— suggested that I might go with them and see slides projected in his house, after tea, I politely explained I'd like to go back to my room and write.

Overload

When I reached Chamu's room in the hotel, his wife, Rukka cried through the bathroom door, 'So you have come! Don't go away. I must talk to you.' I liked the mystery and menace of her tone. The moment she was ready to meet me she said with considerable warmth, 'Did you want to work off a grudge against us by mentioning our name to Mr— of Mysore before leaving? A nice situation you created for us after you left!' I understood what she meant. On the eve of my leaving Mysore, with a dozen things to do by way of getting my papers and baggage in order, a man locally employed in a scientific institution clamoured to meet me although I repeatedly sent word that I was too busy. He said he wanted only a few minutes with me, that he would very much like to say goodbye to his favourite author. No author is so hardened that he cannot be won by such an approach, and so I found for him a quarter of an hour on the day of my departure. I settled him in my study, offered him a cup of coffee as usual, and he told me for exactly the space of five minutes how much he admired my Sunday *Hindu* articles (which anyone may talk about even without reading); and then mentioned his real business with me. He had his daughter and son-in-law studying in a University in the New York State; he wanted me to carry a hamper of condiment, chilli powder and spices, for them. He assured me that the whole thing could not weigh more than a pound, but I excused myself all the same, being an air passenger, explaining that if I had space for another pound I should probably take a woollen sweater or some such thing. He looked as if I had refused to carry some life-saving drug to one in dire need. And so I said (this is where Chamu comes into the story),

'If it is so urgent why not you try and send it through Dr M. N. Srinivas who is coming to the States by boat?'

The man brightened up immediately and said, 'Oh, I know that family so well. His brother was my classmate. His aunt was—was good to us when we were in Kolar, his cousin has married my nephew,' and so on and so forth. He found so many approaches to Srinivas that I felt at the rate of a pound per kinship, he could ask Srinivas to carry a whole shipload of sweets and spices. The next part of the story is best presented through Chamu.

'That man got at me through my brother with whom he renewed his acquaintance. He had been a cricket player once upon a time and you know how my brother melts at the sight of an old cricketer. I told him to send his package along next day. Next day, when I returned home at night I found the passage of our home choking with a wooden chest, the sort of thing the thirteen pirates sat on, a burlap sack, apparently filled with coconut, a smaller trunk containing sweets judging from the swarm of ants, a basket containing possibly brinjals and cucumbers, and three more nondescript bundles. I had come home at midnight from a farewell dinner, and the sight of this luggage upset me. I summoned the man next morning and lectured to him and said that unless he reduced the bulk of his gift to his son-in-law by seventy per cent I would leave it behind. He again started off on how his cousin was married to our nephew, how devoted he was to my cricket-loving brother, how he had watched my Oxford career with pride and satisfaction but I was adamant. He had to take them away. Later in the day they were ready in the passage again, for me. All that he had done was to substitute a steel trunk for the old pirate's chest, the other articles remained unchanged. It was too late to do anything about it now. You may imagine our plight as we lugged all this around, the trouble we had at Bangalore, Bombay, Southampton, London, Manchester, every port, custom, and railway station, porter's tips, vigilance, counting and recounting, in addition to the problem of our own baggage. This trip was completely ruined for us thanks to your introduction, and by the time we arrived at the New York port our patience was at an end; just when we were hoping to be rid of the whole thing we found that the man's son-in-law had not arrived to collect his baggage as promised.The port was in the throes of a dock strike. I had to spend eight hours trying to get help to move the goods to my hotel. Finally I had to dump them in the hotel corridor because they were too unwieldy and large for any normal check room. I wrote to his son-in-law, telegraphed, and finally called him on the telephone, because I was leaving New York but still none turned up, I waited as long as I could and finally left the goods just in the hotel corridor and came away. I don't know or care what happened to them . . . I have only to thank you for all this travail.'

Opiated Cocoon

Picked up by Milton at eleven—lunch with sociologists at Faculty Club. After lunch visit Chicago Museum of Art in the company of some friends, where there is an added attraction of a Sullivan architectural exhibition, mainly photographs of various Chicago and New York buildings.

Sullivan's specialities, such as an arch, a railing, a bracket, a grill, a floral design or filigree on an elevator door, are highlighted. These are viewed as exciting flights of architectural imagination and of daring originality, but do not leave me speechless with wonder, probably because of the odious but inevitable comparison with similar specimens in India in stone and metal which one sees in the ancient temples, and which make these look just casual. But I suppose, it is not right that I should see them in a mood of comparison; my aim should be an 'Absolute' viewing, rather to know what it means to those for whom it's meant. One notices in this country a continual effort to 'build up' tradition in architecture as in other matters— although the tradition may stretch only to fifty years rather than five hundred, and this exhibition is of value from this angle. The conception and execution of sky-scrapers are a daring adventure (here again remember the immense towers of South Indian temples), and Sullivan's work shows sober development in contrast to the eccentric and outrageous efforts of Frank Lloyd Wright. (Possibly Frank Lloyd Wright wants to out do everyone and himself with his recent promise of a one-mile high sky-scraper in Chicago). Quotations from Sullivan expressing his views and aspirations show a lot of feeling for his work, but sometimes sound naive. My own comments on all this may be out of place since I know nothing about architecture, and dare to pronounce them here only because this is my own personal diary.

The whole museum is too big. Extensive collection of paintings, which require a-day-a-room technique of inspection. I could see only a portion of the great collection for want of time and also because I was already afflicted with 'Museum Knees'. But thrilled by the large landscapes by Innes, which are captivating. The modernist collection at the end of the section was exasperating, except one piece entitled 'Rock' which with its glowing colours and exaggerated expressions conveyed some dynamic point of view. Particularly baffling were a splash of pigments on a very large canvass entitled 'The Grated Rainbow', which considering the criss-cross of strands might also have been called, with equal logic, 'The nightmare of an opiated cocoon'. But logic is out of place in this particular gallery, as my friend who brought me here, explained. 'We must not view these with any preconceived set of notions, expectations or habitual attitude of mind'. There was a 'wire sculpture' entitled 'Street Car,' which might logically be also named, 'Balloon Hangers', and another very elaborate, tall one called, 'Family Tree', which started with something like a lobster at the base, and ended with an assemblage of television aerials; it seemed to symbolize (this wretched orthodox habit of mind!) the development of amusement from crab-catching to television or it might have also meant with equal reason skeletons in the cupboard or the need for more hat-stands and coat-hangers in a growing family.

*

At the Quadrangle, Milton Singer comes down to collect us and our baggage at noon. Then a drive to Redfields home 30 miles away, through heavy snow-covered roads, and flurry-curtained air. See a great deal of Chicago on the way. Heavy flurry drifting down like winged ants after a rain and covering the road. Very cold and dim.

Redfields ancient cottage set in a remote site full of trees, now bare and snow-covered—is at the point of the river where the Red Indians crossed into this part of the country in their Westward passage, and the grave of a chief is said to be in the compound left untouched, although once inadvertently dug up in the days of Redfield's father and covered over again. Mr and Mrs Redfield civilized and warm. Their household breathes the utmost charm. Nothing seems to be out of tune here—the mellow Redfields, the timber-beamed cottage, the antique furniture, the reminiscential touches of India in the shape of little bronze pieces on the mantle. Through the window frames the snow covered woods have an unreal postcard picturesqueness. A couple of robins perch outside the window in the bird-shelter, which we can view closely through the glass pane from our side. Abundant conversation, abundant lunch, extreme care being taken not to outrage the vegetarians in the slightest manner—an admirable experience although I am constantly harassed by the thought that we might perhaps get snow-bound, seeing how thick it was falling. We bid farewell to the Redfields at 4.30. Singer drives us back to Chicago, difficult driving on snow-covered, slippery roads.

At six take leave of Singer and his wife at Chicago Union Station. Before parting, Singer slips over my shoulder a camera case. It looks imposing in its leather case. 'Though it looks stylish like a Leica or Rollieflex it's only a box camera. Try to take pictures with it. If you graduate from the box you may go up to costlier ones,' he says. I don't like to be burdened with such contraptions, but he won't hear of it. He insists on proselytizing me to photography.

4

WESTWARD BOUND

On the (rail) road to San Francisco, with Chamu and his wife in another compartment, four doors off. Life in train for the next forty hours. Food in the train, bath in the train, and neighbourly visits to and from Chamu, with many occasions to narrate my new story, and discuss it with him. It is so comfortable that I enjoy having an illusion of being a permanent dweller here, and so arrange my little possessions around on that basis. Find a comradeship with all and sundry,— including the very fat, crew-cut, teen-ager, always tottering with drink. He is a nuisance, as he pushes the door of every compartment in the corridor and peeps in, much to the consternation of Mrs Chamu.

Our life is punctuated by movements to and from the dining car at various intervals—pushing and pulling the heavy doors all along the vestibule. Our biceps are greatly strained. Chamu and I have divided the labour, each doing in one-way. We march along as everyone in the lounge stares at Rukka's colourful sari, with open-mouthed wonder. We notice, however, a red-haired girl and two others being exceptions, who never look up, maintaining a concentrated gaze on their beer glass, all day. The steward is proud of being able to give us rice and butter-milk, and watches over us, as Rukka produces from her hand-bag South Indian condiments and spice-powder to help us through our meals. We form such a close community (although lasting only forty hours) that even the drunken teenager begins to say,

'Good morning,' 'How do you do?,' and 'Excuse me,' every time we pass.

I plan to do some writing but the hours pass unnoticed. I cannot take my eye off the window where grand mountain scenery pass. I think we are passing through an elevation of six thousand feet, farms and towns at night, the beacons on hill-tops look mysterious; wayside towns with their streets, shop-windows, and above all the used-car lots, brilliantly lit all night although the population is fast asleep, and the lights of passing lorries and automobiles on the highway. At some small hour of the night we pass Reno—the haven of divorcees. I fancy I see the sign 'Court' on a building. I cannot help craning my neck to watch if any couple is getting down the steps and parting on the road in silence and tears. But it is an hour at which I suppose, even the turbulence in a divorcee's bosom is lulled into sleep.

Berkeley

Tuesday. Arrive Berkeley. We decide to get down here rather than go up to San Francisco. We climb down by means of a step-ladder. Professor David Mandlebaum and his wife are there to receive Chamu and wife and take us to a hotel. I have a feeling of being an intruder, the real expected guest being Chamu. I have got down here because Chamu is here, otherwise I should have gone to San Francisco and then on to Palo Alto which was really my original destination. But I never get there.

I think Chamu is the luckiest house-hunter in the world. Over lunch at Mandlebaum's he was suggested a house at Albany, a suburb of Berkeley. After lunch David went up-stairs to his study and Ruth drove us to Albany. 1050, Peralta Avenue, (the name attracted us). This was practically to be my second home in Berkeley for the next two months. Rukka saw the house, liked it, Chamu endorsed her view even without looking at the house, on hearsay, and there they were ready to move in as soon as the lady of the house who had recently lost her husband and was going to live with her daughter in New York was able to move her things out. I never saw anyone make such a quick decision about a house. Chamu is a philosopher and a logician, a man who can specify what he wants. I sometimes envy him his clearheadedness and luck. What a contrast to my own management of my affairs. Having decided to stay away at Berkeley, I was next involved in hunting for a flat or apartment for myself. With Ed Harper's help I am engaged for the next couple of days in house-hunting which Berkelians assure me is an exciting, unrewarding occupation. I find an apartment which is available for sixty dollars a month, which figure appeals to me instead of the seven dollar a day for a hotel room. But this apartment is too big, empty, and unfurnished, and I shall probably be obliged to spend all my time like a newly-wed equipping the pantry and bedroom and the front room. I shall have to be thinking all night about sheets and pots and pans, not to speak of grocery, which in any case I shall have to bother about. The heating primitive: you'll have to open a gawky apparatus and apply a match, and when it goes off apply it again and so forth. I never knew that a bare house could look so terrifying and discouraging—all due to its vast emptiness. To add to the emptiness, someone, a weird-looking woman, at the basement, a woman with seven or seventeen (as they seem) children, all in one room, a creaky staircase going up and up, full of thuds. The only reason that such a huge apartment is coming to me for sixty dollars is that the county council has marked it for demolition. Very wise of them. There is a beautiful elm tree in front of the house, which is a point in its favour. There is a spring settee in a landing on which I and Harper settle down to consider the matter. It's a crucial point; if I'm keen on an apartment, this is my opportunity. I shall not regret later that I didn't take it when it came. On the contrary we run over mentally all the things that one would have to do to make it habitable. Out of it a story develops. A helpless man like Dr A—an Indian anthropologist arrives at Berkeley on some important research assignment. He inherits this apartment, and starves for a day or two before he can make a cup of coffee for himself, and a friend like Ed Harper helps him and fills the house with labour-saving gadgets. Dr A—spends his time learning the technique of house running with American gadgets and in tidying up the place. At the end of a month he finds he has not read a line nor written one—no time. He has all along been trying unsuccessfully to learn how to operate a can-opener, how to turn off the gas, and how to dishwash. He is helpless, incompetent and unpractical—until a girl arrives on the scene who is writing a thesis on his work and wants his help to finish her thesis. She starts running his household for him and complications arise.

'How old is she?'

'Twenty-six.'

'How about looks?'

'Charming.'

'Blonde or...?'

'Of course, blonde.'

After this refreshing dream we go out, and Harper drives me to another house—seventy-five dollars a month; which I reject for the opposite set of reasons it's too full of gadgets and articles and equipment, which I shall be responsible for, the owner going away for a time. If I take this house, I fear, I shall become a care-taker, a sort of my man Annamalai, (who guards my Yadavagiri home for thirty-five rupees a month) with the difference that I should have to pay a rent in addition to watching the house.

We come to the conclusion that it's no good deciding on a house in a hurry, and walk back to where Ed has parked his car. In all this pre-occupation with fact and fiction, he seems to have forgotten the parking restriction, and when we reach the car, a long envelope is stuck at the wind-screen—he has a police check, which means probably five dollars fine. 'I generally pay ten dollars a month in fines' he confesses.

Today I create an unprecedented confusion for myself by checking out of my hotel at 2 p.m. I had all my baggage taken down to the lobby, and within half an hour came back to the hotel to ask for my room again. It happened thus. After deciding against the ramshackle house, with Ed Harper's concurrence, I had decided to move to an apartment on Haste, (sixty dollars a month). But at the last moment Rukka mentioned that David Mandlebaum did not quite approve of my taking a room there. When she said this, there flashed to my mind all kinds of defects in the apartment, which I had already noticed through a corner of my eye—its carpets were frayed, its towels were not fresh and were brought in by the hotel proprietrix herself, who also registered at the desk, there were cracks in the wall of my room, the place was full of old people moping in the lounge, the elevator was rattling and grill-ridden, and above all, the address was Haste and Telegraph, which sounded impossible as I feared I might have nightmares of 'Haste makes waste' or people might address my letters; 'Post and Telegraph'. And so I went back to tell them I'd not take the room and came back to my hotel much to the astonishment of my hotel manager.

Evening dinner at an Indian restaurant in San Francisco, our host being Ed Harper. Its elaborate and self-consciously planned Indian atmosphere, dim light, long coats, bogus Indian tunes out of gramophones hidden in the arras, more bogus bric-a-brac are deliberate, but I suppose, commercially successful. Chappati and Indian curry, are genuine and are not bogus. A waitress clad in saree, an usher in a long coat buttoned to the neck, create an Indian atmosphere, which seems to appeal to San Franciscans as, I find, all tables booked, and women dressed in caps and gowns, which outdo Fifth Avenue style, sit with an air of facing an impending adventure, while reading the menu card; and utter little cries of 'delicious, delicious', when they sample a curry. The story of Dr A goes forward in this setting. He decides to find a suitable bridegroom for the blonde—taking a fatherly interest in her (after taking time to realize that he is too much her senior and has a wife and children at home), being a busy-body and match-maker in his own country he has affection for John, a scholarly bachelor and makes it his business in life to 'arrange' a marriage between the two; he casts their horoscopes, compares to see if the stars match; all in correct Indian style; and this imports into United States the first 'arranged' marriage! A promising theme, which I must take up immediately after the 'Guide' is written. After dinner one half of the party returns to Berkeley while I stay back with John and others to see a little more of San Francisco. John takes us to a Bohemian place, where brandy served with coffee is a speciality. There are suggestive pictures everywhere on the walls, lewd sayings in glittering letters—framed gaudily; deliberate joviality, and girls who affect to be intoxicated and throw themselves on all and sundry.

*

John is a linguistic scholar, teaching Hindi in Berkeley, who sought me out a couple of days before at my hotel, offered to drive me around and show me the places of interest. He had spent some years in India and explained:

'When I was in Mysore, Mr— was so hospitable that I like to do anything I can for anyone from Mysore.' He is a gentle, sensitive, civilized and cheerful being. He drove me to San Francisco, over the Golden Gate Bridge at sunset, initiated me into the mysteries of photography with my box camera; and helped me to de-sensitize my first spool of negatives. With my camera he first took a picture of me standing below the Golden Gate Bridge, forgot to turn the film, and handed me the camera and allowed me to take a picture of him under the Golden Gate Bridge on the same film; when it was later developed I saw on the negative two Golden Gate Bridges with a double-headed, four-armed monster standing under it—my first photographic effort. He gave me a supper of Pizza at an Italian restaurant, took me to visit Biligiri, who gave me scented betel nut to chew and suddenly proposed that we go to Oakland to see the haunts of Jack London.

The inn where Jack London wrote and drank himself to death is still there. It is a shack made out of an old boat the entire floor sloping as in a ship's-bar, and the state of cleanliness and furnishing remaining unchanged since the days of Jack London. The waiter is a genuine admirer of Jack London's writing. Beer is served in bottle, and the man explains, 'It's anyway hygienic.' People drink straight out of the bottle as they do on a roadside soda-shop in Madras, tilting back their heads. Faded photographs of Jack London at various stages clutter the wall, and the waiter throws a torch-light on them while he lectures on Jack London's life and philosophy. He (the waiter) also mentions Raja Yoga, Gnana Yoga and Bhagavad Gita. He confesses to being a book-lover, spending all his spare cash and time in reading. He is interested in Indian philosophy because Jack London was interested in it too. He quotes and explains the basis of various Jack London stories. I suggest that he become the narrator in a Hollywood picture on the life of Jack London but he says that his boss nurtures secretly such an ambition himself and so his own chances are poor. When he learns that I'm an author, he abandons the other guests to another waiter and sits up with us. He notes down the names of my books and he sees us off at the door with a simple good-bye; although his routine statement to every out-going couple would be: 'See you in the spring,' and after they say, 'Thanks,' he would add, 'if you get through the mattress,' full of double, treble, and shocking meanings, but no one minds it. And he generally utters this lewd quip mechanically, without any zest as if it were an awful duty cast on him by his boss.

An Encounter

I loafed around San Francisco till 7 p.m. and returned to the Key-Station, in order to catch a street-car for Albany, where I was to dine with Chamu at 8.30.

I paid 45 cents and took a ticket. I asked at the barrier, 'Where do I get the car for Albany?'

'Albany?' said a man standing there. He pulled out a time-table from his pocket, and said, 'There is one leaving in five minutes. Go, go. . . go straight *down* those steps.' He hustled me so much that I didn't have the time even to say 'Thanks.' I was in a hurry. I went down and saw ahead, on the road, two coaches with passengers, ready to start. As I hurried on wondering which of them I should take, two men standing at the foot of the stairs called me to stop, and asked, 'Where are you going?'

'Albany. If that is the bus. . .'

'Where is your ticket?' I held up my ticket. One of them snatched it off, crumpled it into a pellet, and put it into his pocket. These men evidently liked to keep me at the San Francisco station. They were well-dressed, and looked like the presidents of a railroad or a college; one of them looked quite distinguished in his rimless glasses. I demanded an explanation for their arbitrary handling of my ticket but they strolled away and disappeared into the shadows around a corner of this grim building. Not a soul in sight. It was past eight. I dashed back to the ticket office and asked for another ticket of the woman (I purposely avoid the indiscriminate American usage 'girl') at the window. She said,

'You took one now!'

'Yes, but I need another one for a souvenir,' I said. She said, 'You don't get the next bus until nine o'five.'

'Is it a bus or a coach or a train or street car? What is the vehicle one rides in for Albany?' I asked.

'Why?'

'Each time I hear it differently.'

'I don't know, ask there,' she said out of habit and went back to her work.

I went round the station asking for directions. No one was precise. It was surprising how little anyone here cared to know the whereabouts of Albany, only half an hour's ride away. They behaved as if they were being consulted over some hazardous expedition beyond uncharted seas; while the fact remained as any citizen of Berkeley or Albany will confirm, 'F' trains and 'E' trains shuttling between Berkeley and San Francisco wailed and hooted all night keeping people awake.

This station was getting more and more deserted and I didn't want to miss a possible bus or street car—that might start from some unsuspected corner of it. So I went round looking for a conveyance. At a particularly deserted corner, I was stopped by the two men who had misappropriated my first ticket. They blocked my way. I tucked away my new ticket securely into an inner pocket. I was not going to give it up again. One of them grabbed the collar of my jacket and said, 'Let us talk.' The other moved off a few yards, craning his neck and keeping a general look out. The nearer man said, 'Don't start trouble, but listen.' He thrust his fist to my eyes and said, 'I could crack your jaw, and knock you down. You know what I mean?' Certainly, the meaning was crystal clear. I knew at a glance that he could easily achieve his object. It frightened me. In a moment flashed across my mind a versatile, comprehensive news-headline, 'Remnants of Indian novelist near Key-Station. Consulate officials concerned—' I realised these were men of action.

'What do you want?' I asked simply.

The one on sentry duty muttered something in the local

dialect. The collar-gripper, took his hand to his hip pocket. I thought he was going to pull out a pistol, but he drew out a gold watch with a gorgeous gold band. He flourished it before me and said, 'How do you like it?'

'Don't hold it so close to my eyes. I can't see what it is. Take it back.' Yes, it was a nice, tiny watch. He read my thoughts and said, 'I'm not a bum, but a respectable member of the merchant marine. I'm on a holiday and have been gambling. I want money. Take this.'

It was of course an extraordinary method of promoting watch sales, but I had to pretend that I saw nothing odd in it. He said in a kind of through-the-teeth hiss,

'I don't like trouble, that's all. See what I mean?' His hand still held the collar of my jacket, and the watch was sunk within his enormous fist. It was very frightening. The lub-dub of my heart could be heard over other city noises. I'm not exactly a cowardly sort, but I am a realist. When I encountered a fist of that size I could calculate its striking force to the nearest poundal. I have always weighed 140 pounds, whatever I did, whether I starved or over-ate or vegetated or travelled hectically. My weight never varied. I felt, in my fevered state, that the man before me must weigh as much between his fist and shoulder. No police in sight. The entire force seemed to have been drawn away to meet a graver emergency elsewhere. I looked casual, as if it were a part of my day's routine, as if someone were always turning up doing this sort of thing to me every two hours. I tried to assume the look of a seasoned receiver of ladies watches. The whole scene filled me with such a feeling of ludicrous staginess that I suddenly burst into a laugh. The man looked puzzled and annoyed.

'You think it funny?' he asked.

'S-u-r-e,' I said in the most approved drawn-out manner, dreading lest my tactics should misfire. He gave a tug to my jacket. I said curtly, 'I hate to have my jacket pulled. I hate anyone hanging on to my jacket. It shows an infantile mind and mother-fixation'.

'You are a professor, aren't you?' he said sneeringly.

I asked, 'Whose is that watch?'

'My own. I would not be selling it otherwise.'

The other man turned round to say, 'It is of course his. Should you ask?'

'I don't believe it,' I said. 'May be you are a guy with a slender enough wrist to wear that strap. Let me see. how you manage to put it on! Seems to me it's a lady's watch.' At this he repeated his threat about my jaw. I had by now got used to hearing it; and almost said that if he broke one jaw another was sure to grow in its place. I still marvel why he didn't hit me. I took off my spectacles as a defense preparation. I didn't want splinters in my eyes. He ran his hand over the entire surface of my person, trying to locate my purse. Ignoring his action I repeated emphatically, 'It's a lady's watch.'

'It is Pat's,' said his friend.

'Who is Pat?'

'His wife,' he said.

'What does she do now to know the time?' I asked.

'I got her another one', he said, 'that's why I want to sell it.'

'Does she know about it?' I asked.

'Sure. Peggy will do anything to help me.'

'Peggy?' I asked. 'Who is she and how does she get on with Pat?' I asked.

'What are you talking about?' he growled. We had now arrived at a level of conversational ease which must have looked like the meeting of three old school-ties around the corner. The only unsavoury element in it, if one peered closely enough, was that he still had his fingers firmly on my collar. He assumed a menacing tone suddenly, and asked,

'So you don't appreciate our help?'

'Thanks a lot I don't. You are really mixed up. Your wife, if you have one, must be either Pat or Peggy, not both unless you are a bigamist who lets two wives manage with a single watch, or am I going to hear about Sally and Jane too? Are you a bigamist or a polygamist? Are such things allowed in this country?'

'Oh, stop that, you talk too much; that's what's wrong with you. Jack made a slip, that's all,' the man said with a touch of sadness.

'What's your time now?' I asked. 'I've a dinner engagement at Albany—' He looked at his own watch. He applied it to his ear and cried, 'The damned thing has stopped.'

'No wonder,' I said. 'All that clenching and flourishing of fist will reduce any watch to pieces,' I said. 'Why don't you look at the cute one in your pocket, Peggy's is it?' He pulled out the little watch, peered at its face and said, 'Can't see anything in this blasted place.'

'Why not we all adjourn to a better lit place?' I suggested.

'And have a drink, eh?' he said.

After Jack had his laugh at the joke, the other one said, 'Professor, you are a good guy; learn to use an opportunity. You don't appreciate our help. Do you know what this watch actually costs?'

'Do you?' I asked.

He paused to think up a reply. His friend, Jack, turned round to say, 'It cost him one hundred forty dollars,' without taking his eye off the corner.

'What's your offer?'

'Not even the twenty cents that I am left with now,' I said. 'I would not accept it even as a gift. You know why?'

'Why, Doctor?'

'I've no faith in watches. I never wear one; I've never had a watch in my life. Only recently, for the first time in my life I bought a two dollar alarm clock, because, every morning I slept till twelve noon, and was in constant danger of missing trains and planes. So now I have a clock, which I strictly look at only once in a day; just to know whether I should get out of bed or continue to sleep.'

'How do you keep your appointments?' he asked.

'I never keep them. I should have been eating a dinner now at Albany. But where am I? What am I doing?'

'Now you know we want to help you.'

'I'll never buy a watch even if I miss all the dinners in the world,' I said emphatically.

'Perhaps you should take this to your girl friend,' he said.

'No such luck. Never had one in my life,' I said. 'Even if I had one, I'd never inflict a watch on her. It's a misleading instrument. What's a watch-time? Nothing. You don't even know how to look at Sally's or Pat's watch in your pocket. Your watch has stopped; I'm sure Jack's watch is showing some wild time of its own. It's a different hour now at New York; something else in Chicago; morning time in the other hemisphere, Greenwich Time, summer time, and God knows what else. What's the use of having an instrument which is always wrong by some other clock?' He looked overwhelmed by this onslaught. His fingers slackened on the collar of my jacket, and I took the opportunity to draw myself up proudly, turn, and briskly walk away, with my heart palpitating lest they should grab me back. I walked off fast.

I don't think I overcame them by my superior wit and escaped. I cannot claim any heroism on that score. I think they let me go because they must have felt that they had caught a bankrupt and a bore. Or it may be Jack espied the police somewhere and they let me go. Although I missed my dinner that night, I was glad to be back at my hotel with my bones intact; and as long as I stayed in Berkeley, I took care not to visit the San Francisco Key Station again.

Sunday Excursion

Half the Sunday spent in finding my way to Chamu's house at Peralta Avenue in Albany. In this process came across a number of places with picturesque names, such as Euclid, Scenic, Cedar, Spruce, Sonoma, Pomona, Carmel. Felt tired. Finally managed to reach Albany. Mrs Chamu was good enough to keep rice and curry and curd for me. Evening John came down to take me for the *Diwali* celebrations at the International House. I resisted going there at first—afraid of the air of fraternity. But yielded for want of a better occupation. A number of dances—sketchy and extremely amateurish. The usual ingredients of Indian cultural fare were there: wicklights, vague, slow, plaintive and drawn-out music, women clad in saris going round each other gently swaying their arms, interspersed with definitely crude stuff such as Hindi film-hits played on harmonica by two youths (which seemed to appeal to the audience more than anything else); phoney folk-songs in languages nobody knows, and all the distance from the home country could not excuse the performance, considering the big, eager crowd that had turned up. Speech by the Indian Consul. The air was so heavily, deliberately Indian that I felt oppressed and persuaded John to come out. An American standing in the corridor, wearing a South Indian dhoti, jibba and khaddar cap (style of any waiter in a restaurant in South India)—and pointedly refused to shake hands, when I stretched my hand, but performed a *Namaste,* showing off perhaps his familiarity with India, where some foundation must have taken him to learn him this trick. I don't know whether it's hypocrisy or ignorance, that makes them do such things. Where is the point in mimicking a piece of Oriental courtesy when you perpetrate occidental bad manners by ignoring a proffered hand? We went to the campus book-store for browsing—always a most desirable proposition.

*

At the book store John met a friend—a Dr Schurman, an expert in Chinese, Japanese, Arabic, who proposed that we adjourn for a drink somewhere. He drove down-town in search of 'Lemon and Cat' or some such well-known 'quiet' pub. It was as usual dim-lit, 'atmosphere-ridden', but so full that we had to get out again and search for another place; finally he drove us to his flat, where he could provide us fruit juice and beer. I was impressed with this man's knowledge of Eastern languages. For light reading he read Chinese literature in the original, and Greek and Hebrew when he wanted to bite into harder stuff. Being a woeful failure at learning languages, not knowing any except Tamil and English, I was definitely impressed and wanted to proclaim that he should be the grand moderator in the Tower of Babel. We dispersed at midnight.

Picked up by John at noon, and then on to Chamu's for a South Indian lunch. Chamu, the saviour! After lunch, John drives us over the Berkeley Hills, Tilden National Park, Grizzly Peak, and Red-wood forests, till sun-set—all through wonderful mountain scenery.

I was getting obsessed with the thought that I was not putting my camera to good use. So brought it out today and exposed a few rolls—delicately framing each picture around huge elms and redwood, and with Chamu, wife, and John in each spot. I took so much time to compose each picture that the others became impatient. I begged them to stand still. But unfortunately I forgot to readjust the shutter from where John had set it for time exposure under the Golden Gate Bridge the other evening, and so no one turned up in a recognizable shape when the films were later developed; thus lost a chance of immortalizing the magnificence of the scenery and company that we enjoyed that afternoon.

End of a Quest

Another day of house-hunting, having firmly decided to stay in Berkeley rather than at Palo Alto in order to write my novel. Scrutinizing of advertisements in *Berkeley Gazzetteer,* following up hearsay accounts of apartments available; thanks to Ed Harper's help visit the University housing centre, and tell one Mrs Keyhoc (I could not concentrate on business as my inner being clamoured to know if 'KEY HOLE' was being mis-spelt) that I almost belonged to the university faculties before she could take an interest in the proceedings, and then she telephoned a number of places and gave me a list, very reminiscent of Roser of Anta in efficiency and thoroughness; she gave me an impression of running everyone down to earth. 'Here is a man who wants a room for writing with kitchen facilities, private bath, prepared to pay etc., etc.' She would pour forth into a telephone. Finally we march out with a list in our hands. My preference is for Albany because of Chamu's proximity. In Albany we do go to a house owned by an old Japanese lady, who knows absolutely no English and who is feeding several noisy, scraggy dogs, the apartment upstair is good but without bed or blankets, to be provided by myself. Sixty dollars a month. I am delighted with the prospect and as usual almost promise her on an impulse that I'd take the flat and come and occupy it next day. Edward Harper drops me at Chamu's and goes away. After dinner Chamu's wife phones the news to Ruth Mandlebaum and they all come to the conclusion that it would be madness to pay sixty dollars for bare apartment without bed or utensils, and they remind me that the apartment I declined the other day had everything for sixty and yet I wouldn't take it! And then the fundamental question whether it is worth living in far-off Albany for Chamu's sake or in Berkeley with all the amenities around. I feel hopelessly lost. I have already a feeling that I am going to let the dog-loving Japanese lady alone. We sit discussing several prospects, but come to one conclusion that I should quit my hotel as it takes away seven dollars a day while I spend most of the day in the streets looking for food and shelter. I return to my seven-dollar hotel in a taxi, my mind full of problems. Get off at the bookstore. While browsing around the campus bookstore I suddenly look up and notice Hotel Carlton staring me in the face, never having noticed its presence before. Walk in and find Kaplan, the manager, extremely courteous and full of helpful suggestions—he's willing to give me a room where I may use a hot plate for cooking my food, daily room service, separate bed and study, ideal in every way, the perfect hotel for me. And it costs seventy-five dollars a month.

Check out of the seven-dollar-a-day hotel at two and check in at Carlton at five minutes past two next afternoon. That very night acquire an electric hot-plate, a saucepan, and rice, and vegetables, and venture to cook a dinner for myself. Profound relief that I don't have to face again the Cafeteria carrot and tomato fare!

For the first time a settled place where I don't have to keep my possessions in a state of semi-pack. I am able to plan my work better. I am enchanted with the place, everything is nearby, two cinemas, three or four groceries, and any number of other shops, I can walk down and buy whatever I may need and peep at the Campanille clock to see the time, its chime is enchanting.

Palo Alto

Mrs K—is good enough to drive me to Palo Alto thirty miles away. Nice in everyway but for the restless presence of Joe, her five-year old son who talks too much and often blames his mother for monopolizing all the talk and so they come to an agreement. Joe to shut up till such and such a place is reached, and his mother to shut up till they are in such and such a place. Joe to do the talking when we arrive on the bridge. You know how interminable San Francisco bridges could be, and Joe exercises his right of chatter and refuses to recognize that the bridge is past. A duel goes on between the mother and the son, and it is the mother who appeals for a truce each time; the result is that our conversation gets to be extremely jerky and incoherent, full of interruptions; add to it the strain of driving at sixty miles an hour keeping an eye on the lane, watching the route. Children should recognize that elders have generally the right of way in talk, and a little firmness in handling them will go a long way in avoiding conversational chaos. The lady confesses that she is no good for the strain of such a long drive, but had ventured out today because of a hope that she might talk to me on the way. But unfortunately this cannot be realized. Between the strain of watching out while driving, and keeping Joe satisfied she has no chance of saying anything worthwhile, and when we arrive at Palo Alto she turns me over to Robert North and goes away for over an hour out of a delicacy of feeling that she may perhaps seem intrusive while I confer with North.

I had mistakenly thought that Robert North would be upset over my choice of Berkeley instead of the original plan to stay at Palo Alto and that I might have to be apologetic, but he seemed relieved that I had settled at Berkeley. He announced, 'This is a place where you can't get a house or a hotel room.'

I feared he might want to hold me at Palo Alto at least for the evening but he merely said, 'We must have lunch together, some afternoon. I'll find out about the time from one or two others and call you—.' I could understand Mr North's pre-occupied condition. At his study you couldn't flick a finger without knocking down a pile of books and papers. He was surrounded with a mountainous quantity of reference for writing (if my impression is right) a study of the political developments in the East. He looked overwhelmed by the amount of material he would have to wade through.

I could not say I cared very much for Palo Alto either. To me it was like selecting Srirangapatna for a prolonged vacation; and so when Mrs K—returned to drive me back to Berkeley, I was ready for her.

In all this, nearly a hundred miles drive up and down, one

saw automobiles moving in a string, at nights like an endless torch-light parade, up and down the Bay bridge, along several lanes, but not a single pedestrian to be seen anywhere, nor a dog, nor a cow, nor a tree. This gave it all a touch of grim, machine-ageness (one of H. G. Wells' nightmare visions). The pedestrian has been successfully liquidated on the Freeway which may be defined as the most mechanized patch on earth.

'Phoneme'

I find Biligiri most fascinating. A brilliant student of linguistics, always dreaming of his girl in Mysore. One who looks both rugged and sensitive at the same time. He gave us all a dinner at the Mexican restaurant, run by a Goanese who has married a Mexican woman—truly a marriage of culinary experts. The food was very Indian and very enjoyable. Only after the dinner my hosts could think of nothing more stirring than a lecture on phonetics by a visiting expert. I went along with them and took my seat in the hall.

As I listened I was appalled at the dryness of the subject of phonetics. The Professor read a paper supressing a yawn all the time in the mumbling rapid manner of a nervous secretary reading an annual report. I didn't follow a word of what he said; I caught 'Phoneme' or 'phoney' constantly. The audience sat through in dead stillness; in a state of morose resignation. The only sentence that came near to making any sense at all, was some quip about making a Synchronic approach to Diachronic studies; which stirred the audience to a brief fit of polite laughter. I felt that I had wasted an evening in sitting through this baffling function: everyone pretended that the lecture had been too simple and elementary and not at all what they expected of such an eminent expert. Even if the men had really understood this lecture, what about their wives, who rallied in good number and sat through as if it were an after-dinner entertainment?

Visit Biligiri. He has paid five dollars and bought a fancy notebook, gilt-edged and bound in real cow, with ivory pages. He takes it out of its case and shows me the poems he has written on its pages—an offering to his sweet-heart. He reads me one of the poems in Kannada. It is entitled 'Neenu' ('You' in Kannada), and says 'In the thorny thicket, that is my heart, appeared a rose that is 'You'. . .' etc.

After dinner picked up by John to join a party on the Hills at Ed Harper's. The view from the hill is beautiful several times magnified view of Mysore from Chamundi at night. I find the party itself unbearable. Bunches of anthropologists, all talking simultaneously and no one listening in particular, drinking and filling the air with smoke.

At a cocktail party men and women arrive who don't care for each other or for the function, hold glasses which they would rather throw away, sip drinks with an air of doing so under compulsion, say things which are inane, utter remarks which no one hears. Everyone shouts at the top of his voice, and contributes his mite to the general din; no one should stand apart and look out of the window. He must munch monkey-nut, wash it down, and contribute to the babble, smoke, and confusion.

I looked about and saw Chamu engaged in an earnest conversation with a young professor, in the quiet seclusion of the fire-place. I approached them with a feeling of relief at finding someone to talk to; but they stood with their backs to the assembly and were engrossed in their own talk. I overheard Chamu say, 'Tell me, do the Australian Aborigines correlate copulation with population?' I asked Chamu later why he should bother about the question. He said, 'Oh, anything to keep his mind engaged. Otherwise, he would have bothered me to explain the caste-system in India.'

Nothing much to record, the same routine, I have got into the routine of writing—about one thousand five hundred to two thousand words a day anyhow. I have the whole picture ready in my mind, except some detail here and there and the only question is to put it in type. Some days when I feel I have been wasting my time, I save my conscience by telling Kaplan at the desk, 'I am going to be very busy for the next few weeks trying to get on with my book.' A restatement of purpose is very helpful under these circumstances. Graham Greene liked the story when I narrated it to him in London. While I was hesitating whether to leave my hero alive or dead at the end of the story Graham was definite that he should die. So I have on my hands the life of a man condemned to death before he is born and I have to plan my narrative to lead to it. This becomes a major obsession with me. I think of elaborate calculations: a thousand words a day and by February first I should complete the first draft. In order to facilitate my work I take a typewriter on hire, after three days of tapping away it gets on my nerves, and I lounge on the sofa and write with my pen. Whatever the method my mind has no peace unless I have written at the end of the day nearly 2,000 words. Between breakfast and lunch I manage five hundred words, and while the rice on the stove is cooking a couple of hundreds and after lunch once again till six, with interruptions to read letters and reply to them, or to go out for a walk along the mountain path, or meet and talk to a friend.

Telephone from Chamu to say that his neighbour, an elderly man, who often used to invite him to watch the Television died suddenly of a heart-attack while shaving in the morning. Chamu and his wife terribly shaken. In the United States death sounds unreal. The man had said 'How do you do?' from the road as I was waiting for Chamu to open the door on the previous evening. Chamu's landlord had also died similarly three months ago. So a feeling of insecurity about Peralta Avenue itself.

With John and Biligiri, to an Italian restaurant to eat Pizza: but the atmosphere was spoilt by a debate between me and Biligiri—who was also a severe, uncompromising vegetarian like me, but who somehow protested against my statement to John that I was a vegetarian because I didn't like to kill for food. He asked whether we didn't kill the vegetable world for food to which I said in reply with heat that we don't generally uproot a tree for eating its fruit, which he hotly debated. He became very gloomy and remained silent for the rest of the day. (I fear he is very homesick and has had no letter from home.) After dinner they went to hear a lecture on linguistics, but John would not take me along, probably for fear that I might behave frivolously or utter loud, cynical remarks at the meeting.

More Joint than Food

Lunch with South East Asia Group–imposing name, actually consisting at the moment of John, Ed Harper, and one or two others.

Ed Harper, talking to another, entered the lunch hall, at great speed with an air of one not knowing where he was going. They were preoccupied with Joint Family. I heard them say, 'The Joint family is . . .'

'No, I want to know its structural. . .'

'It is like this. The members—I mean the agnates—the whole thing is . . .'

'According to the original matrilineal scheme . . .' With all these idioms on their lips they approached the lunch table and took their seats. The subject was interrupted for a tenth of a second by a 'Hallo', to me as they suddenly remembered I was their guest. One of them leaned over to ask,

'Oh, here he is, let us ask him . . .' and they demanded 'Can you define Joint Family?'

'Of course, I can, being a member of one,' I began. 'You see it's like this, a father, mother, and sons, and then the sons and their families, all under the same roof . . .' Before I could warm up to my subject they lost interest. They turned away and were completely lost in their own talk. They kept gesticulating and talking all through the course, now and then pausing to draw a chart of Joint Family organization on an imaginary sheet of paper on the table. There was someone on my right who made a few desultory observations on India—most men here had been to India and knew some aspect of it. With their preoccupation with joint family, my lunch reduced itself to a small plate of fruit salad. Providing a lunch for me is a complicated business at any time, but it is rendered more difficult when my hosts become preoccupied with the evolution of Indian Society. After they left, I went back to my room, cooked a lunch for myself, and I could take a more generous view of the South-East-Asian group after my rice and curd at four in the afternoon.

Versatile Bob

I must pause to say a few words here about a young man whom I shall call Bob—. I received a telephone call one night. 'This is Bob—of the U.C.L. I want to interview you for our paper.'

'Which is your paper?'

He said something that I did not quite catch. I gave him an appointment for next day, when there walked into my room a young man biting a long piece of carrot. He had the usual dress and deportment of a college student: crewcut, pull-over, and some odd trousers and a bundle of notebooks under his arm.

'I am doing features for our Daily Californian, and I want to write a feature about you. I have written features about Christopher Isherwood, Aldous Huxley, and Henry Miller, I drove down to Los Angeles and saw them. Isherwood says that he writes only for his own satisfaction and that he doesn't think of his public while writing. Do you agree with his view?' I said something, and like the reporter at Michigan, he searched for a paper in his pockets, found one of the size of a bus ticket, and then vainly rummaged for a pencil, and gave up the idea of jotting down. He asked, 'Is this your first visit to this country? How do you like this country? What are your impressions?' I answered something briefly and then asked him, 'What made you come to me?' He had no ready answer for me. He merely said,

'Mr Harper told me that you are a novelist from India and so . . .' I asked him how much he knew about my books. He knew nothing but asked,

'Are your books available in English translation?' I felt it would be a strain to launch on an autobibliography. I gently turned the talk to other matters. I asked,

'What do you plan to do after you leave college?'

He said, 'Well, I am hoping to become a journalist. I am a feature-writer for our college paper, and they are very popular. I am married. I have a little son four months old. I and my wife live a sort of joint family life with my aunt who has a big house.' At the end of the interview (mutual) he said,

'I have a car, and I would like to drive you to San Francisco if you wish to look round there . . .'

'Why should you take the trouble?'

'I enjoy driving people. . .also if you would like to see Henry Miller I could drive you to Big Sur . . . only a hundred miles away. Shall I write to him and fix an appointment? He was very kind to me.' When he was leaving I asked him, 'How will you write the feature, I didn't see you note down anything?' He said that he had a good memory and that he could write this interview out of his head; he also requested me to give my candid opinion of it when it appeared at the end of the week, and he also offered to send me cuttings of his other published features and confessedat the end, 'I want to write a novel during the vacation next year.' That was the last I saw of him as a feature writer and journalist. Next I met him a fortnight later outside the grocery on the Telegraph. He had as usual a bundle of class-books under his arm, and was munching pea-nut (he must be one of the steadiest customer for the picturesque ice-cream vendor who stations himself at the Sather Gate ten a.m. to five p.m. every day crying 'Crunchie-Munchies, yes come on, buy 'em, eat 'em, them's good for you') Bob's mouth was full as he tried to say, 'Good morning, my car is over there, I have parked it at Dwight Way, because no parking here at the campus. I am off to Palo Alto immediately. I have a new assignment for which I have to refer to old newspaper stacks at the Hoover Institute. I am particularly interested in seeing old copies of *The Times of India*.'

'Really? Why?'

'I am going to study the matrimonial advertisement columns in the paper so that I may get an idea of the trend of the caste system in India for the last thirty years.'

'How will you be able to get an idea of that?'

'I hear that matrimonial advertisements are popular in India and people mention what castes they prefer or no caste restriction and so forth. I am going to note it all carefully so that I may get a picture of the breakdown of caste system in India.' Next time we met, Bob was in the lobby of my hotel. One morning, weeks later, he telephoned me from the desk as I was struggling with my two-thousand-words-a-day of my new novel. I went down to speak to him for a moment. This was the only occasion when he was not chewing. He must have had a surfeit of snacks. He said,

'I have just finished my examinations, and I want to know if you would like me to drive you anywhere, sir?' I thought over it, still sixty-thousand words to write. I'd not have peace of mind anywhere outside my desk. 'I have no time, my boy. I will call you whenever I am free.' I could not resist asking, 'What are you interested in now?'

He answered like a shot, 'I have taken Russian Collectivism as the subject for my thesis.'

I left him at that and had no occasion to see him again. I look forward to seeing the result of his versatile activities in due course, provided I knew in which walk of life to look for him at a given time.

T.V.

I've become a Television addict. Every evening I rush through my quota of writing and prepare my dinner in order to go down to the lobby and sit down with half a dozen others and watch the television, which goes on till 11.30 in the night. I have no peace of mind until I know the latest progress of the sixty-four thousand dollar question or seen a full-length film of other days. Kaplan generally informs me if there is a special programme—'Nehru is appearing in a programme at 11', or 'Ed Murrow's special interview with—' and we finish our dinner and crowd the lobby. I return to my room at 11.30. It is diverting but it spoils one's reading habits. If I have to read, it can be only after Television—that keeps me awake till 1.30 or 2 at night.

The Television personnel exude 'prosperity'—aggressively cheerful, relaxed, homely, confident, assured, and knowing what you want and what others need—in cars, cosmetics, food, cigarettes, and cleansing agents. Their perpetual smile is of Paradise,—their gleaming hair, teeth, and knowledge are of a superworld.

Luckily for us Advertisers have not learnt the technique of projecting themselves and their ideas into our dreams; not the day ones but the night ones, when we are asleep and may completely be at their mercy, if only they knew how to reach us there telepathically.

*

'Hutchi' (a Kannada word) meaning—the 'crazed woman', is the name of Ed's cat. It's just like any other cat. But they like to think that their cat is slightly touched in the head. Watching it, it did nothing more than any other cat. But it's a fashion, I suppose. Remember the French girl at Madison who held the gathering spellbound with an account the madness of her various cats, and how she took them one by one to a psychiatrist, because her husband was positive they should be psychoanalysed and so forth. It's an affection. Edward also said that a cat he had in Shimoga would behave all right till orthodox brahmins came to his house for a conference in the evenings, when she'd bring in half a mouse and toss it in their midst; outraging the pious assembly. Proves the devilry of cats.

The Unforgettable

California is a state where 'morticians' abound, where mortality is constantly kept before one. On a public bench you cannot lean without reading the inscription on the back-rest, 'No-flame cremation is our speciality. Calcification is the latest form of disposal.' Or one may read on a corner hoarding, 'Bring us your funeral problems. Sympathetic responsibility is our motto.' Or 'Funerals undertaken on easy-instalment plan.' In this atmosphere, I grew dejected when I discovered one morning a drop of blood coming down my nostril. It completely spoilt the day for me. Could hardly manage to write fifty words for the day; became a prey to all morbid thoughts. Should I leave instruction at the desk, 'If my door is not open when the room maid calls in tomorrow, please get in touch with Chamu whose telephone is—?' Spoke to Kaplan and felt comforted to know that nasal congestion was common in this part of the country. Later confessed my worries to Chetty and Biligiri, who confessed that they too had this trouble. Greatly relieved. It is good to know that all Indians coming to this country bleed at the nose first six months!

The word 'Prosperity', has almost a religious compulsion

about it. An anthropologist friend of mine asked me, with reference to India, why we fought shy of Prosperity, and why Indian philosophical thought was opposed to it, how anyone could avoid prosperity or set a limit to it?

A car for every third person is prosperity. And then an endless creation of goods, and their sales. And so a vast advertisement programme starts. Its urgency, because of competition, is so great that it invades every medium of communication. At first you may naively think what a wonder Television is. But alas, it is only a sales-medium. Every programme serves only as an excuse for sandwiching messages about haircream, cigarette, soap, and automobile; health, wealth, wisdom, and happiness, according to the character on the Television screen are to be attained only by inhaling the smoke of such and such cigarette which has the distinction of having fifty thousand filters (whatever it may mean, but it prevents lung cancer about which the medical profession has chosen to make so much fuss)—all adjectives are used in support of it, all music is subservient to it, and all acting, personality, dramaturgy, is a message-bearer.

In times of War all talent is pressed for propaganda. In peace all talent (the television could make the highest bid) is pressed for sales promotion.

I feel a violent jolt when a narrator who earns our respect otherwise suddenly interrupts his performance to step aside to say,

'I want to tell you about the cigarette which I most enjoy smoking. It is . . . remember . . .' and then he spells and repeats it. Or the tragedienne of classic dimensions suddenly goes off to say, 'You may wonder why I care for . . .soap . . .' and then goes on to spell the name of this profound soap. Perpetration of such a violence to the sacredness of artistic illusions makes one furious—out of that fury the following scene is written:

One Continuous Mood

SCENE: (Dark night. A lonely cottage. Wind whistling outside. An old woman is warming her soup over the fireplace.

Knock on the door).

O.W. (Old Woman) : Who is it? At this unearthly hour.

Voice: Sh! Sh! Open the door, matter of life and death!

O.W.: I won't open the door.

Voice: Please, save my life. Don't delay. (Distant baying of hounds). There they are. Open the door. (The old woman shakes her head and tries to go on with her soup).

Voice: By the way, I can hear you drinking your soup. Remember one thing. XYZ soup is reinforced with vitamin B14. It is the only soup with vitamin B14. Remember it. B14 will knock the years out of your age.

Voice: (As the baying of dogs approaches) Good Woman, do you like to see my body mangled at your very doorstep?

O.W.: No, go, go away, do not disturb me. (Suddenly the dogs are right at her door. Several voices are heard. She listens intently to the various sounds. She pushes away her soup bowl, wringing her hands.) Perhaps he really needs help . . . Oh, God save that poor man! (She tiptoes to the door, and with her hand on the latch pauses for a moment and says:) My hands are soft because I use only Gopi Flakes for laundering my linen. Gopi also can wash your silks, your sink, your utensils, your walls, your furniture, floor, carpet, shoes or automobile. In fact, Gopi is right for any cleaning job. Gopi cleans twenty-five times faster than any other detergent and costs five times less. Remember Gopi is the only one which has Blimol in it.

(At this moment the man outside hurls himself against the door and crashes in. The old woman is thrown off, but luckily supports herself by putting her hands out and catching the wall.)

O.W.: What do you mean by this?

Visitor: (Who has a cloak around his head) I am sorry, terribly sorry. I will repair your door for you.

O.W.: (Surveying the man) Who are you? Are you a thief or a renegade? You look fierce enough with that beard of yours.

Visitor: (stroking his beard thoughtfully and finally taking it off) you see, it is false. My enemies are after me.

O.W.: You may rest in that corner.

(Darkness falls on the house; the man sits hunched up at the door waiting for his friends. He falls asleep and wakes up at dawn. The old woman enters.)

O.W.: Oh, you still here! (The visitor wakes up and yawns.)

Visitor: One reason why I prefer Watterrwet Towels is that they are soft, soft like the petals of a rose. They are in seven pastel shades—one for each day of the week, packed in—. (He flourishes a glittering package.)

O.W.: I have to go out for a while. (The old woman picks up her mop and bucket.) Watch that kettle. Take it down when the water boils.

Visitor: I will. (At this moment, clatter of horses' hoofs is heard. The old woman has just opened the door.)

Someone outside: Who is inside?

O.W.: (Trying to shut the door) No one.

Horseman: He must be here. Do you know who he is?

Horsemen: The rebels are busy pillaging the palace. They have announced a price—on Your Majesty's head. Let us rush away. (The old woman is aghast on hearing the word 'Majesty', and kneels down.)

Visitor: (Giving her a ring) You have been good to me. Keep it. Goodbye, I must go now. (The men march out and get the horses ready. H.M. rushes out, but pauses at the door to say:) There are three reasons why I prefer Stonebreak Soap. First, it is the cleanest soap in the market. Two, it is the only soap which can make your worn-out skin glow again, and three, it never slips through your wet fingers.

(More horsemen arrive).

King's friends: (Cry in unison) We are lost, they have found us. But we will fight. (Swords are drawn. It is difficult to see who is who in this melee. You hear the clash of swords, and groans of the wounded as they fall to the ground.)

O.W.: Ah, bloody sight! in my poor cottage! (She edges her way to where the King is fighting with his back to the wall. She carries the kettle of boiling water and pours it down the neck of the man who has cornered the King; the man leaps up. The King knocks him down, kneels over his chest, ready to run his sword through him.)

King: If you are thinking of a nice birthday present for your daughter, give her a Sissy Tractor, which is the only one with a built-in Dish Washer. Run it on your field; it'll plow the earth.

Set it up in the kitchen; it'll wash your dishes. No down payment, no up payment. In fact, no payment at all. Take the tractor, use it, when it's worn out, bring it back and we will give you another. Remember, for your child's birthday, a Sissy Tractor!

Fallen man: Take away your sword. I'll tell you.

King: Yes, speak.

Fallen man: About your children.

King: (With sword at his heart) Oh, what about them? Tell me, tell me soon.

O.W: (To the audience) Bad breath is instantly abolished if you use Breatho pills; the cost works out to 1/4 cent each hour. It's the most scientific antiodour pill ever made.

King: Oh, tell me about my children. Are they safe?

Man: They were intercepted, and they are now in our custody. If you do not surrender before mid-day they will be . . .

King: Oh stop; don't say the word.

Man: I know where they are. I'll take you there.

King: And also collect your reward; you will get your reward and I shall lose my head, h'm?

Man: (Embarrassed) I suppose so, Your Majesty. For that headache that never stops, take Pancita 606. Pancita 606 gives 32 times faster relief than others. (The old woman bursts into tears. All the Kings followers go out mutely. The man leads the King out gleefully.)

King: All our yesterdays have lighted fools their dusty way to death. One word more. Porcupine under wear keeps you cool in summer and warm in winter. Look for Porcupine underwear wherever you go.

Post-Mistress

Post Mistress at the Berkeley Post office, while registering my letter: 'Gandhi! What a great man! Himself so simple, but helped the people to raise their standard of life. He created a bloodless revolution—like the Christian revolutionaries during the early years of Christian era. I've heard friends say that Gandhi was a devout Christian too. Have you states and districts and counties in your country? Population 400 millions, that's a lot of population! Must be hard-pressed for space, isn't it so? What's the area of your country? We've a 100 million population in this country, but a lot of waste space in between everywhere! . . . The charges would be 46 cents—give me a penny, I'll give you a nickel for the 1/2 dollar. Penny! is a survival of our British connections you know. We are one with you there: actually we are cousin-like because we both got rid of the British.'

'Bew-da'

Religion is not a thing that anyone can openly avow—it's like one's underwear. You may make oblique reference to it or joke about it. At the Cocktail party in Lyla Jacob's house, biochemists and such from the science department of the University, and a couple of Indian students who would not betray their traditional outlook. You may joke about God, but that's as far as you should go in civilized societies. 'Ambedkar, author of Indian Constitution is dead—'

'Did he not convert one million Hindus to Buddhism?'

'What's Buddhism?'

'Followers of Buddha.' (Pronounced 'Bew-da' or 'Booda' in this country).

Someone—'I am all for Buddhism—'

'What does it oblige one to do or imply?'

'Nothing. You are just a Buddhist–that's all.' One of the scientists—sat rolling his eyes and parodying religious attitude, quite grotesque in a man usually grave, mumbling ,

'Oh, I'm the Buddha—I see him there,—I hear a knock on the door,—they are coming up—I prophecy there is a female coming—Buddha in female form . . .'

Just nonsense. And then they talk about monsoons and earthquakes.

'Funny feeling when there is an earthquake.'

'How does it occur?'

'Well, God is supposed to bear the universe on his little finger, and when he changes it from the right to his left—there is an earthquake.'

'The world is borne on his head;' and someone mimed the action of such a God as he lifted the burden off and on. Laughter.

Lyla: 'I think it could just as well be that—simplifies everything. Why not so?'

Scientist: 'Nice way to explain everything. If you say God, you don't have to explain anything. Plenty of hypotheses, unquestionable basis for conclusions, you can stop half way through an argument or data and put the rest on God. No notes or step-by-step calculations. What a saving! If I could have him in Bio-chemistry Research, it'd save us so much labour!'

'I saw Martin Luther—it was good. It seems they'd to stop a Television Programme of it in Chicago.'

'I wonder how Catholics could tolerate it even at the beginning. . .'

'How can the word of God written three thousand years ago, be a fixed factor? 'Thou shall' or 'Shall not' may sometimes have to be elastic . . .'

'I hope there is no Christian here,' said the scientist after another performance of God-miming. Irreverence, Blasphemy, are here as compelling a creed as any religious practice in a monastery.

*

Half an hour with Kaplan at the Desk, discussing the fate of old people in this country. Carlton full of them, grand parents thinking and talking to each other of their sons and grand-sons, and waiting all hours at the lounge, hoping for a letter or a meeting at weekend. I was touched by the old man who brought for a show around the framed photo of his grandson who held two large fish he had caught. The boy had bowed his head as he held the two large fish. The old man almost lifted him in the picture by the chin so that we might see what a fine smile he could display. He explained that the boy's modesty made him look down, and so called the picture, 'Modesty in achievement,' much to the approval of the erect, deaf, 90-year old man who moved on measured steps all day, and who remembered India, when he was in Calcutta in 1912;—'I'd a watchman, outside my bedroom. I had bearers all over the house—I wonder what

India is like now?' This old gentleman told me that he was writing a monumental work on the philosophy of common-sense. He advocated in the book the test of commonsense for all problems—and it is sure to abolish not only war in the international field, but also divorce. When any conflict was imminent one had only to ask, 'Is it commonsense?' and the problem would have a ready solution. He had split common-sense into practical, manageable, doses and had examined its application, in personal, family, state, national and internation-al problems. He said that he was busy on it all day preparing the final copy with the help of an editorial secretary. As we were talking, beside the glass door, people were passing in and out, but he noticed no one—his mind was all on commonsense. I was duly impressed with the possibilities of his work and its application, until he said,

'I'll send you an autographed copy of my book before you leave.'

'But,' I said, 'Your book is not yet printed, is it?'

'No, one or two publishers have asked for it, but I'm still working on the manuscript.'

'How can you promise me a copy? I'm leaving in two weeks.'

'Not impossible,' he said, 'in these days when we have such good printing machinery.' So I left it at that. He looked so earnest, I had not the heart to contradict and argue with him as to how a book could be set up, printed and bound, and be ready to be autographed in fifteen days; especially when no publisher had yet seen it and the book was still unwritten.

*

Mr Woolfe: 'Countries are arming themselves to the teeth, and when that happens, history has shown us there is always a war. This part of the country is particularly bad to live in if there is a war—with its cyclotron, navel-building yards and so on. The thing to do is to quit this place. If there is a war, I'll be the first to quit. If you find a sudden gust of wind blowing in at the door and someone asks, 'What is that storm?' you may say, 'It's Woolfe clearing out of San Francisco.'

*

'Hi! Professor!' said the active and ever-busy, ever smiling scholar also a permanent resident of our hotel, whose name I never learnt, but who mentioned one night that he was working on the history of ideas—and knew Greek, Hebrew, Latin, French, and many other languages, and who was also able to fix up the television for Woolfe, when something went wrong with it. He always greeted me with 'Professor!' and a nod, whenever he saw me. My convocation and the conferring of an honorary doctorate on me by the staff and fellow-guests of Carlton deserves a whole chapter by itself. Shortly no one need be surprised if I print my cards as Doctor N; I have so got used to being called 'Doctor' or 'Professor!' by all and sundry.

*

The Guatemala lady whose son is in a hostel spoke to me in whispers at the lounge.

'This whole American life is based on getting rid of parents. I sent my boy to the Berkeley college and planned to take a house and run it for him. But the university would not hear of it. And so he has been in a hostel for a year now. Already I see him changed. He does not care for me. No respect for mothers!' I have discussed all this with Kaplan, who agrees that family life should become broader and include others beside husband-wife-child unit. People should become less self-centred. He said improvement in nutrition and public health, has produced longevity, which has resulted in the presence of a lot of old people retired from family and profession as permanent residents in hotels because a son when he marries likes to live independently, and a modern house is so built that except the immediate family no one else can dwell in it without becoming a great nuisance.

'So, I think the solution lies in building houses with an extra suite for parents, built in such a way as to afford them privacy and independence. So, the fault is with the architects' I say.

Metro is of the view that the old people themselves are responsible for their present condition. 'They want to be either totally independent as in a hotel room or totally interfering if they are with their off-spring. They are a troublesome unaccommodative lot.' Nor does Metro seem to approve of children. He called them an unmanageable nuisance in this country. He suspected that unnoticed they were gradually forming themselves into a 'pressure group' in this country.

Metro bowled me over by asking, 'What is the real difference between Hindus and Muslims?' I began to say, 'Hindus write left to right and Muslims right to left. Our auspicious days are inauspicious to them, Hindus venerate cows, while Muslims feed on them. Hindus don't mind the pig, while Muslims abominate them. Hindus worship idols, while Islam forbids idolatry.'

Metro listened to it all and said, 'Still I do not see why it should lead to fighting and blood-shed.'

'That's true', I said.

'So what is the real difference between Hindus and Muslims?' he persisted and I had to say,

'I don't know.'

*

A couple of mornings ago an old man, standing on a pavement at Channing Way, who watched me hop across the road avoiding a Volkswagen remarked when I reached him,

'Bad enough even if it's a small car that runs over one,' and then he asked,

'From India?' followed by 'I've a daughter in India.'

'Which part of India?'

'Madras.'

'Madras! Where in Madras?'

'Her husband is in the State Department in the Information services'.

'Name please?'

'Tufty.' I was taken aback. What a coincidence to run like this into Mrs Tufty's family. I explained how well I know the Tuftys, how they gave a party for me when I left India, no longer than a couple of months ago, good friends of mine. The old gentleman was overcome with emotion;

'The world is a small place indeed,' he cried.

'I had been thinking only today how far away is my daughter—It's a far off world for us, but what a joy and relief to meet you, you bring that world so close to us. Please come for tea and my wife will be so happy to meet you.

*

Metro was also an author living in this hotel. He had written a novel of over one hundred and twenty thousand words, working on it for five years now. He had a room in Carlton, and a job as a night clerk four nights a week at a hotel in Oakland, which gave him enough funds to maintain himself at Carlton, where he was completely lost in composing and chiselling his novel during all his spare days and hours. He showed me a few chapters and I found them rather strong—too much blood in each chapter; overloaded with corpses in deep-freeze, and blackmail, million dollars changing hands, and fast driving. He had taken courses in fiction-writing, studied books on the subject, and worked unswervingly on the theories he had learnt. But still something was wrong somewhere as he himself felt that there was too much beating-up, and the speeches of his characters sounded to his ears vapid and impossible. He asked for suggestions. I could only say that he should cut down the length by half. He considered my suggestion until he was able to see my own work; I lent him my copy of *Waiting for the Mahatma* which he read at one stretch and returned to me saying, 'I think the book is weak in motivation, we don't learn anything about Mahatma Gandhi, and the narrative lacks punch.' And thus my criticism of his own effort was set off, and he felt less unhappy as he realized that I was after all a writer of weak motivations, and with probably no theoretical knowledge of fiction writing. Apart from this difference of views, we often met and went out to drink coffee and talk literary shop.

*

Having written the last sentence of my novel I plan to idle around Berkeley for a week and then leave on my onward journey. I have lived under the illusion that I would never have to leave Berkeley. Berkeley days were days of writing, thinking, and walking along mountain paths, and meeting friends. And so, when the time comes for me to plan to leave, I feel sad. How can I survive without a view of the Sather Gate Book shop, the chime of Campanille clock, the ever-hurrying boys and girls in the street below, the grocer, the laundry, and the antique shop? I shall miss all those musical names of the streets—Dwight Way, Channing, Acton, Prospect, Piedmont, Shasta, Olympus, Sacramento. I shall miss all those scores of friends I have somehow managed to gather. I shall miss Lyla's voice on the telephone. When the sun shone the telephone was certain to ring and she would say, 'Isn't it a beautiful day?'

David Mandelbaum invited me to tea on the eve of my departure. Ruth had just read the *English Teacher,* and I could see how she was overwhelmed by it. She wanted to ask so many questions about it, but could not. David told me later that the book had a disturbing effect on her mind. In the hope of lightening her mind, I gave her a copy of *Swami and Friends*.

The whole of Sunday busy cancelling my original plan to leave on Monday. The whole of Monday spent at bank counter, baggage forwarding agency, and the telegraph office. Late in the evening Biligiri dropped in. John came to ask if he could drive me to the airport next day, but the Vincents have already offered their help. Ed Harper came in with a box of candies to announce to me, Indian style, the birth of a son.

Frantically busy morning, because I have still not completed my packing. John and Irene Vincent come to drive me to the Airport. Kaplan at the desk becomes sentimental of my leaving. John Vincent carries my bags all through, in spite of my protests. They come up to the last inch of the barrier, and hand me a hamper of fruits and candies before saying good-bye.

5

LOS ANGELES

LOS ANGELES at six p.m. Arrive at San Carlos. Find the room rather small—and I am not able to find a grocery store nearby. Eat sandwich for dinner and stroll down Broadway.

*

By bus to Venice to see Mrs Dorothy Jones. A critic and serious writer on filmatic values, especially valuable is her study of Hollywood's treatment of foreign themes, which she did under the auspices of the Massachusetts Institute. More than all, her helpful nature and knowledge of film studios and personalities, made it easy for me to visit the film world. Met her at 6 o' clock in the evening at her house in that far off place. Over an hour's journey by bus right through the heart of Los Angeles. The magnitude of Los Angeles could be realized only in such a journey. The word 'sprawling' is uttered the moment anyone thinks of Los Angeles, and one could understand the epithet now. Venice is nearly at the other end of the town and searching for Glyndon Avenue on foot, proved an interesting way of familiarizing oneself with this vast city. The types of faces one encountered were all different from anything one saw in other parts of the country, starting with the gallery of old men at Pershing Square; and the Bible lecturer haranguing them '. . . I can have all the wealth in the world. But I don't want it . . . I know God gives me what I want. . .' and so on. 'I'll tell you about the Holy Ghost. . . Recently the wise men of

California said that if a certain oil company should cease, the town would become a ghost of itself. . . But this holy ghost is not a ghost like this threatened oil town . . .' He was clearly going off the rails, nobody in the least minding it. They paid no more attention to his lecture than they did to the pigeons hovering around and cooing. . .

*

Tomorrow I'm going to make notes on the road of the bearded and other extraordinary personalities one comes across on the road. Women of tremendous beauty pass along in the crowds—and the men all look suspiciously like film toughs, and deliberately cultivated picturesque characters. A newspaper vendor near my hotel looks like W.G. Grace the old English cricketer with his beard and peaked cap . . . He has begun to call today's evening edition, already stale, 'Thursday morning edition,' and recommends while I pass him, 'Read it; you will be well-informed if you read tomorrow's morning edition, that's what it is actually!' It is about nine in the evening. Tomorrow is still far off. Is news printed ahead of occurrence? I wonder!

*

I must definitely give Milton Singer's camera back to him because I'll never photograph anything. The very idea of photography detracts my mind from watching any scene or situation with a free mind (as a writer). I start worrying how it will look in the view-finder, and am seized with the regret that, as usual, I've left the camera behind, or that I've carried it when there is no sun and so forth. It's all a useless preoccupation. Every place sells picture post-cards, and that should be sufficient for my record, and the photographs are so much more competently taken!

*

First time in my life purchased a clock at the corner drug store. Bought a big one for one dollar odd, kept it on my table for five minutes, went down again and returned it, and bought a smarter one costing a couple of dollars more. 'For an extra dollar, sure you get extra value, sir,' moralized the store assistant. I bought this just by way of precaution against unpunctuality with regard to various engagements ahead. At the Carlton (Berkeley), I could peep out and read the time on the Campanille tower, but here I could see nothing but dark, sooty walls when I looked out; and the view was always better curtained off.

By virtue of possessing the time-piece got up early, arranged my affairs tidily so that I had cooked, dishwashed, and was ready to meet Mrs Dorothy Jones at eleven-thirty. She was very helpful. She drew up a list of persons for me to see at Hollywood, and sat at the telephone and filled up my programme book with the address and telephone number of each person. When she saw that I had a tendency to note my engagements on loose paper she presented me with a small pocket diary, and for a start put down all my engagements in it, and handed it back to me with, 'Don't forget to look into it, first thing each day.' Drove me to Hollywood, searched far and wide, and fixed a room for me in a motel on the Sunset Boulevard as a first practical step, as my down-town life at the hotel did not have her approval. After this a drive-in lunch and we went to the United Artists Corporation. Met Sidney Harmon (Security Productions), said to be a sensitive playwright and high-brow producer. He asked me a number of questions about India—from geology, population, down to individual daily life, and asked what exactly was the difference between Indians and Americans. But I have grown used to questions and never rack my head to find an answer, as from experience I find that most persons (like the Jesting Pilate) don't wait for an answer. He asked me suddenly what he could do for me at Hollywood, and when I told him I'd like to meet a producer interested in an Indian subject, he went on to dilate on the quick-sand economics of the film, listed all the good films that proved a failure since the beginning, and finally talked himself into the conclusion that it would never, never pay, and nothing would ever pay in films. He quoted enormous statistics and spoke, he said, as a businessman. The recent success of the Giant seemed to have brought a lot of confusion and rethinking in all their production plans. One would think a big success would make everyone feel more encouraged but I've noticed film producers are afflicted with mixed emotions when they see any picture become an abnormal success. They call a halt to all their own plans, telling each other, 'One can't survive unless one gives the public another Giant.' For a moment I was oblivious of my surroundings not really knowing whether I was listening to any of our own movie moguls in Madras, Coimbatore or Bombay. They have all the same idiom, eloquence, and monologous tendency. They will set aside everything else to be driving home a point with 'You know what I mean . . .' 'You see what I mean . . .' with brief (and sometimes prolonged) interludes into the telephone. I liked Sidney Harmon and he promised to take me to the sets tomorrow. Dorothy suddenly remembered that she had to get back to her children and started off at four-thirty. I found my way back down-town by bus. Returned to my hotel and started out again to buy food-stuff. Found as usual all the grocery shops closing. This was the third evening in succession that grocery was unavailable. Returned to my hotel to find a call from Dorothy, who gave me for my diary noting a number of engagements for tomorrow. I've to pack up and be ready to leave at noon tomorrow. Dread the prospect of packing again. Anyway time to leave this hotel—the traffic noise is getting on my nerves, and my room is so dark that I don't know whether it's night or day.

Dorothy phoned to say she would come at one in the afternoon. Frantic packing and cooking—two activities for which I am, by nature, unfitted, but which are on me all the time. For brief half hour went out to visit the library on 5th street. It's a magnificent place on several floors with millions of books in every language in the world. At the information hall on the second floor (first floor in our reckoning), the lady pointed out to me the huge murals on the walls—showing the discovery of the coast and the founding of Los Angeles. Here and there on the niche were kept Egyptian relics of thousands of years gifted by a local collector. Went through the fiction department and saw *The Financial Expert* and *Grateful to Life*—the copies looked well thumbed and their issue cards were crammed with entries.

Hollywood

Afternoon occupy the motel on Sunset Boulevard according to plan. I'm now right in the heart of Hollywood. Call on Mr Geoffrey Shurlock, Vice President of the Motion Picture Academy who has taken over the functions of the old Hay's Office, and applies the Production Code to new pictures; he is concerned with the censoring of scripts and reels. He flourishes on his desk, The New York Times Book Section as a thing he studiously follows and claims that he is familiar at least with the reviews of my books. He asks about Indian films and I mention *Avvaiyar*. We have many other topics coming up but at four-thirty Dorothy remembers her duty to her children—Kelley must be picked up and then her husband at his office and we leave Shurlock. She puts me down at the library of Motion Picture Academy, which attempts to collect all literature and documents concerning films, a very thorough, comprehensive library, where one may read the accounts of films of half a century ago and all the press cuttings connected with them. I glance through an album presented by Richard Barthelmess (of Little Lord Fauntleroy) of old days, containing press-cuttings of his performances; including a letter of congratulations from Mary Pickford on the day of his marriage, in her own hand, with envelope preserved intact. A waft of history; the dust of time has settled down on many things here. Hollywood is already building up a past, creating a tradition, and, I think, rightly too considering the shattering impact of Television at home and the trade restrictions abroad, and the general economic morass, in which, I'm assured by everybody, the trade is grounded at the moment.

Aldous Huxley

'Take the bus No. 89 at Hollywood and Highland and come along to the very end of the line—Beachwood Drive, I'll come and take you in my car,' Mrs Huxley had phoned last night. At Hollywood boulevard, I got into the bus 89. I asked the driver, 'I want to drive to the end of the line, what's the ticket?' 'Where do you want to go, Pal?' he asked.

I showed him Huxley's address.

'H'm. We go all the way down Hollywood Hill. Whatever is beyond is yours to manage, O.K.?'

He took me in with resignation—a cheerful soul, more talkative than anyone else of his kind, I've seen. He told a lady, who had failed to get off at the right 'transfer' point,

'Learn to know your bus, honey.' He also spoke to girls adopting a thin piping voice: with all this entertainment, I did not notice the passage of time and felt sorry to part when he stopped at a place and said turning to me, 'Well, this is all, Pal; I go back now.'

It was the beginning of a hill-road with a drug store and laundry, and a post-box. A number of cars were arriving, driven by women, myself always wondering which of them might be Mrs Huxley. As I sat there on a bench outside the store, a tall, handsome, old man, looking like Francis Ford of the old days came up and sat beside me and started talking. He said, pointing at the granite bastion at the entrance to the hill road, 'There used to be guards posted in those days to keep off peddlers and others whom we didn't want here . . .' History again within fifty years! When he learnt I was from India, he said,

'Your country! A great job it's doing to keep the peace of the world. But it's a mad world—people don't want to live and let live, that's all. . . How Britain exploited India and other countries! I'm a Canadian. Canada is the only country in which Britain's tricks did not work, although in World War I and World War II, they made us the front line in every battle! . . . I suppose they did the same thing with India too! Sixty years ago I fought . . .'

I had to leave him. 'Excuse me!' I said and abruptly went off to look for Mrs Huxley, who, I feared, might be looking for me. Very soon a small car came up—Huxley recognized me, and brought the car down to my kerb. He got out of the car asking,

'Have we kept you waiting?' Recognition was mutual and instantaneous. His house was on the hill. As we entered his gate, there was another car standing, and he said, 'I've asked Alan White of Asiatic Studies at San Francisco to lunch. He is an oriental scholar, you'll like him.'

At the drawing room, the furnishing and upholstery was all white, with glass windows bringing in light—(I suppose in order to help Huxley move around without difficulty on account of his sight). He took me to his patio and pointed out the magnificent valley ahead. He pointed out to a pot of foliage: 'it's just sweet potato—which has just burst out in such foliage isn't it amazing!. . .' At lunch I knew he had to divide his talk between the other guest and me. They had terse references to works on Mahayana and Hinayana Buddhism, and he was rather surprised at the revival of Buddhism everywhere—and wondered if it was partly a political strategy. We spoke of Gandhi (Otto Preminger had once consulted him for a possible film of Gandhi); Industrialism, and he asked many questions about India. Mescalin and the opening of the doors of perception, were of course extremely recurring subjects. After the other guest left, he took me into his study—full of books and letters, and an uncovered typewriter.

'Perhaps you may want to rest?' I asked.

'Oh, no, I don't rest in the afternoon. Stay on, I may go down later and let us go together, if you do not mind it.' I had mentioned *Gayatri Dhyana Sloka* earlier in the day in connection with his own thesis on colour perception as an aid to Yoga. He wanted me to say more about it. I explained *Gayatri Dhyana Sloka* and the *Mantra* step by step, and suggested he might find more of it in Arthur Avalon's writing. He took down several of Avalon's books from his shelf and wanted me to show him the exact place where reference to Gayatri could be found. I couldn't find it anywhere just then, but I promised to write to him later about it.

'What books are now being published in India on Tantra? Are the theatres very active? How is the younger generation? Are they conscious of their cultural traditions? No? What a pity! When two nations get together they get the worst of each other—Rope-trick and such things from your country and gadgets and mere technology from the West! Isn't it extraordinary! A most fantastic piece of history. Britain's one hundred years association with India—a company going and settling down and creating all kinds of problems at that distance! Under Mescalin, a single bar of music lasts a whole eternity. I'm not a born novelist. It does not come easily to me. I've to struggle and work hard to get it out—not like Balzac for instance through whom it just flowed;—the novel form is wonderful if you can achieve it. As we grow in years, it becomes more difficult to write a mere novel—all meditation technique is just to open up our own layers of consciousness and experience—to feel the richness of awareness and not for any particular achievement or results. . .' He quoted Blake.

'Yes. . . the Perennial Philosophy helped me a great deal in understanding. I'm glad I wrote it.'

Calm, gracefully slow, and careful in movement, lean and very tall, with a crop of hair, which younger people might envy, perfectly shaped nose, and lips—it's a delight to watch his profile: his hands and the long tapering fingers; a check jacket, and corduroy trousers, and the hand-knit tie, gave him a distinguished appearance. I sat talking in his study till he said he was ready to go out. Before starting he brought out his new volume of essays, 'Perhaps you'd like to see this—, well, the first two essays are good, I think.' He drove me down-hill with a promise to telephone me again. 'We must get together again before you leave,' he said.

*

Spent the Sunday in Dorothy's home at Glyndon Avenue, Venice. Kim, Kelly, and David the youngsters were wonderfully active. Jack, Dorothy's husband, was relaxed in an absolutely Sunday mood. They put the chairs, rough, wooden ones, out in the yard. They showed me their guinea pigs, the fat cat, their parakeets. They thanked me one by one for a box of candies I had brought them. Jack, not a very talkative man, told me that his association with India was when he passed Madras coast at a distance of 30 miles during the War and saw a ball of fire shooting across the horizon—to this day this phenomenon remains unexplained to him; and at Colombo they got down and searched for beef-steak, a guide promising to help them took them to a restaurant where they palmed off lamb as beef!

Afternoon they became quite active building up a fire for Barbecue—father and boys, running hither and thither and setting it up. Sally Simmons–Dorothy's friend dropped in; she was full of knowledge, observation, and curiosity. Her hobby was watching crowds and characters. She knew Hollywood (of normal life and people not of films) inside out. She declared that Hollywood was no longer what it was reported to be—it had ceased to be anything different from a normal town. It was a centre of oil business, aeronautic construction, and electronics, rather than of mere films; all the studios had moved outside Hollywood proper. We sat round talking, eating, drinking, and watching television, and it was eight-thirty p.m. when Dorothy drove me back to Hollywood. Before I left little David brought me his file of stories—he wanted to be a writer. I blessed him and hoped he would be a writer with a Book of the Month honour one day, much to the delight of his dad, Jack.

*

Visit to Sam Goldwyn studios, arranged by Dorothy with Sidney Harmon. At three o'clock I was there. The routine phone-up from the reception desk and so forth before the portals could open. Since I was a little earlier, I waited in his office. Harmon's Secretary, a smiling, cheerful creature, offered me coffee without sugar or cream. She explained,

'It's really very good coffee, you know,' endorsed by another visitor waiting with a portfolio under his arm. It encouraged the girl to explain,

'You know, why it's so good? I make my own blend and kiss every grain. . .'

'Well, in that event, I think I'll try it even without cream, you seem to have given it the right treatment,' I said, and tried to enjoy the decoction.

'Are you hungry?' she asked next.

'No,' I said.

'I have a packet of salmon-sandwich which I can give you.'

'Why don't you eat it yourself?' I asked.

'I'm dieting. I don't want to grow fat.'

I did not ask what made her carry around sandwiches, which she didn't intend to consume. I just said,

'You don't look the kind that'll grow fat, but if you are destined to grow fat, no power on earth or in heaven can help you.'

'We Americans eat too much,' said the other visitor, and demonstrated it by offering to help the girl out of her salmon-sandwich load.

Meanwhile the room was getting crowded with sleek men, and elegant women, all of whom nodded and said to me, 'How do you do?'

I am too experienced in the film world to take too much notice of anyone or offer my seat. It's a free-and-easy world, where there is a lot of relaxed, mutual indifference, and the courtesies of the humdrum world are neither missed nor noticed. I carried on the same technique when Sidney Harmon whom I was waiting to see, who had been so warm and communicative two days before and had said I was to ask him for anything I needed in Hollywood, came out of the room. I just continued to sit and look away at a pretty girl who had emerged also from his room, a few minutes before. We might have been total strangers for all it mattered. He threw a brief glance at me and muttered a word to someone, and passed out of the room. I never saw him again. A new person (Public Relations?) came on to me with a fresh smile.

'Please come with me. Let us go down to the studio.'

'What about Mr Harmon?' I said, suddenly feeling that Harmon was slipping out of my ken.

'Yes, sure. He will meet us later. Shall we go down?'

'Sure!' I said catching the spirit of the hour.

We were presently passing on to a stage crowded with people. The moment the door was shut behind me, I might, for all it mattered, be in Gemini Studios—the same groups of people—half of whom too tense and half too relaxed. Suddenly my guide put his finger to his lips and cautioned. It was as if we had stepped into a cave where a tiger was asleep. The tiger here was a temperamental director of whom every one seemed afraid. . . At a corner of the studio they were shooting a scene with Burt Lancaster and Miss Simmons. The cameraman was pointed out to me in respectful, nervous whispers, as an academy winner—a Chinaman, with his thick glasses and five-foot height who looked so much like Ramnoth, (of Gemini Studios at Madras) and moved about like him. It made me regret for a while about Ramnoth, a good friend and a film-associate for years, of whose death I had learnt from a newspaper, which I opened in the plane while leaving India.

The man who guided me slipped away after handing me over to another, who spoke to me for a while, and slipped away in his turn, with a 'Make yourself comfortable'. I watched the endless rehearsals and preparations for the shot and found it was all the same the world over. The Director was high-strung and kept saying.

'Silence, gentlemen, someone is talking. . .' like a class teacher, and every one giggled at the fuss he made and tried not to creak their shoes. I noticed on the set a property which intrigued me—Nataraja in bronze. . . ubiquitous God, whom they pick up and carry about like some savage visiting a city and picking up an electric lamp (without current or wiring) for a display in his jungle home. To see Nataraja, the Shiva of India, included in the setting for a Chinese story, being made in Hollywood, seemed to me a grotesque but perfect international mixture. I slipped out in my turn and went back to my hotel without a chance to say 'thanks' or 'good-bye' to anyone.

Evening dinner with Sally Simmons, and then a drive, which she had arranged with an automobile owning friend of hers. We went up the hill to the planetarium and saw half this country stretched out below, and then here and there nearly fifty miles of driving looking around Los Angeles. We ended up at a famous ice-cream cafe in the university village which offered seventy different ice-creams. The menu card displayed a list of all the film and literary celebrities who had tasted the ice-cream. While leaving, I saw at the doorway, a niche in the wall and a very large Ganesha in white marble kept in it. Where did they get it from, the god from a distant land, blessing this ice-cream bar with prosperity! I told the manager, 'Wherever you may have got it from, he is a god, Ganesha the Elephant-faced (because, oh, that's a big story in our mythology), who is the remover of impediments, and giver of prosperity; you probably owe your popularity to His kindness— apart from the quality of your own service.'

Unloved

Visit the famous Universal International Studios. Lunch with William Gordon—head of the international section, who feels disturbed by the attitude of Indian Government, who were understood to be hostile to Hollywood in general. Nothing disturbs film folk so much as the thought that they are not loved and admired. India Government somehow averse to Hollywood. Mr. Gordon projected for me Bengal Brigade, which was refused a certificate in India. No use attempting to find a reason for the refusal since the Government itself had not given any. The producer had gone carefully through the script changing all words likely to offend the Indian sentiment—such as 'caste', 'Get out you low caste', was changed to 'Get out, you low class', but it had sounded to my ears, 'caste', until it was explained to me; in any case it didn't matter materially since the word caste is by no means a tabooed expression. Why, why was the Government of India so inimical to Hollywood? I couldn't say. He took out huge files and showed me all the correspondence. The picture was not certified by Trinidad, Indonesia and Hong Kong, countries, which somehow, accepted India's leadership in such matters. The nations of the world seemed to be marshalled against Hollywood. It was nice sitting in that well-furnished office and listening to all these problems. In no other walk of life do people arrange their office equipment so stylishly—the poorest film producer will have at least four coloured telephones and all kinds of table equipment, which the President of a Nation might envy. Mr. Gordon proved that India was a loser in the long run as every film producer interested in India would bring it at least two million dollars into this dollar-starved sub-continent. It was all high economics which I didn't quite follow. Ultimately Mr Gordon hinted, that if the Government continued its unfriendly acts, Hollywood would be driven to making pictures of India uninhibited, faking all the background in Hollywood, stories wildly misinterpreting India, which would certainly create box office records all over the world. I said, 'Why not?' Instead of worrying over Delhi attitudes.

*

Visit to Macgowan, head of the Theatre Art at the University of California. At first he mistook me for a visitor from Pakistan whom he had been expecting. He looked confused and bewildered by this slip. Personally I didn't mind. I see nothing wrong in being thought of as a Pakistani as long as I am not questioned on politics. He phoned his next in command to come up and join us. Before ten minutes were over I had collected an armful of departmental literature. The next man came up and kept the conversation going. He took me round to see the departments, handed me over to the director of cinema-teaching and disappeared. This man, Richard Hawkins, proved a valuable friend. A deep friendliness abiding for three hours. I have lost all value for the duration of friendship, as long as it is good, while it lasts. He showed me his film department; and then said that as he had particularly nothing to do at the moment, he would like to drive me around in his car. He took me up the hills all the way, and down to the ocean, and along Will Rogers Avenue, across the city, and all the way around and finally insisted upon driving me back to my hotel. He had been driving for over three hours continuously, a quiet, gentle soul, full of sensitive film values. Thanks to him I saw the entire Bel Air area, more aristocratic than Beverley Hills, Santa Monica, Will Rogers Beach and some of the hill locations of old-time movie chases on horseback.

*

At two o'clock Walt Disney studio with Dorothy and her son Kim. A guide met us at the Reception, and for the next two hours, he explained everything in that fifty-six acre ground, with its twenty-six buildings and one thousand five hundred employees, working to entertain, amuse, and make money. Television, movies, magazine publications (eight million total sales in various places of the world) articles of amusement for Disneyland. How many things! How many! What co-ordination! It took six years to make a picture; one million drawings made for a feature. Shot frame by frame through a stop camera. Fundamentally, it depends upon a single individual, on the creative work of an artist. The animator actually draws pictures for every stage of movement, arranges them one under another and flicks them with his fingers muttering the dialogue and syllables in order to synchronize sound and picture. To help them in this work all the dialogue is completely recorded first, and played back. The colour store, fantastic combination and numbers—made by Dupont (seventy odd primary colours, made into two thousand by combination), the 'Cel' painters, girls, with their own radios and earphones to while away the tedium when their hands colour-copy. A place where genius, creative play on a large scale, toy-makers spirit on a large scale, expert organization, technology, business, specialized engineering all combine. It's so crowded and so much organized that it made me wonder if there was space for Disney himself to do anything in. Our guide assured us that his spirit pervaded the place,—when he passed with a nod or a word, he set his stamp. He was unseen, but like God he was pervasive. I wanted to ask which God ever possessed such a business acumen. I was told that Disney's brother managed all the business. The odium of commerce is on the other Disney, not on Walt.

Shurlock brought his car and took me to the Huntington Library and Picture Gallery at Pasadena—a most attractive place, (Huntington was a rail-road President) with its green lawns, and park-land, looking like an English country side—names also, such as Euston, Wembley, Oxford and so forth. Huntington Library—where one saw Chaucer and Shakespeare first editions, Caxton's original, and ancient etchings, wood-cuts, and illuminated manuscripts, and the art gallery with Gainsborough's Blue Boy and Lady Turner and various other pictures one has heard of all life.

Reserved

The famous cemetery, made famous by Evelyn Waugh's Loved One, the Forest Lawns, was the next place of visit. A whole mountain converted into a burial ground by a big business organization. Flowers on picturesque tomb-plates, lordly avenues, churches, statuary and spacious lawns, meadows, and arbours—verily a place where one might live rather than be dead in. The speciality is that you could drive-in and lay a wreath. I saw one or two mourners pulling up their motor-cars beside their loved ones and laying flowers (supply of which is also a part of the business organization) on the horizontal tomb-plates. The tomb-plates do not stand out but lie flat along the sloping ground because they save space (which is the real sale-commodity here, selling the dead space to be dead in) and do not disturb the perspective. The plates are of metal with the names of the dead engraved on them with a nice cavity in each for sticking flowers as in a vase. Everything is provided for here. Under these Grand-hotel-like perfection of arrangements there is no time to feel the pangs of bereavement. The sting of death is removed by business foresight. I noticed also school children picnicking in various corners of this attractive retreat. Ever since I entered California I had been seeing gigantic notices hitting one's eyes everywhere, '. . . 110 dollars assure a place in Forest Lawns', which I had taken to be some sort of Save-Our-Trees-and-Lawns campaign on a state-wide scale. Now I understood that these were only advertise-ments of cemetery-space. The view of the city from the hills quite inspiring. At the massive iron-gates, offices of Life Insurance companies too! Geoffrey wondered how these two businesses were compatible!

And then he drove me to the Hollywood Bowl, an open air theatre, which can accommodate twenty thousand at a time, on the mountain side, where concerts are held in certain seasons with parking space for twenty thousand cars. And back to his flat—stopping on the way to see the 'Tar-pits' at a public park, where natural tar is oozing on the ground, where Indian cattle path lay, and where they have dug up an immense quantity of pre-historic fossils. Back to Shurlock's room on the eleventh floor looking over the entire city; where he made coffee for me, and we spoke of Indian castes, Gandhi, and Gita and so forth. He showed me a copy of Gita in translation which he has read for years. Dinner at a cafe. And then he took me up a mountain to show me the city view at night. We parted at eleven p.m. He must have driven me over one hundred and fifty miles today showing me the sights of Hollywood. He'd not let me thank him because he said he could not have seen

Huntington Library but for me; he had been planning a visit to the Huntington Gallery and other places for about thirty years, and could achieve it only today. Great soul, silently suffering— having lost his wife three years ago; in his lovely flat on the eleventh floor, surrounded with music, books, memories and a view of the city,—he tries to forget himself in his work as a censor. He is one of the most lovable and popular men in Hollywood, although, in his position he could easily make himself odious to everyone.

Aldous Huxley

Another afternoon with Aldous Huxley. As usual they came down to meet me at the bus terminal. Huxley took me for a walk to show a few places on the hills and a lake, an artificial one, which is supplying water to Hollywood, pumped up all the way from Colorado, nearly one thousand seven hundred feet up as he explained. He explained at length various statistics about water supply, his mind is really encyclopaedic, storing up all sorts of facts and figures as one notices in his latest book. I have left a copy of *The English Teacher* for him to read. I explained to him some of the psychic phenomena in it, and told him about the lesson Paul Brunton taught me years ago. He explained that he was trying almost a similar experiment, but would like to try the suggestions in my book too. He cheerfully takes up any mental experiment suggested to him. We talked of Forest Lawns and he said, thinking it over, that it's so colossal and detailed that it's past the stage of being laughed at, where there are chapels, but no crucification, no cross, no suffering; only the Last Supper, but not beyond—a place where a discreet censorship is applied to death, so that no pain or suffering is indicated—these are not to be remembered; but death only as a happy holiday—even adding a sort of glamour to it, as a sort of inducement to book a space in Forest Lawns; chapel where recorded hymn goes on; and marriages take place immediately to be followed by a cremation. 'In this country,' Huxley said, 'You come across fantastic things side by side. At one place you'll see a huge advertisement for Forest Lawns, next to it whisky, health food, and gambling at Las Vegas, probably also some religious activities, and something else. Well, consume whisky and ruin your health, or gamble and blow yourself out or think of God, but the end is the same in any case may be the underlying philosophy in all this. You found things rather jumbled up, in this country.'

Mrs Huxley said when we returned home,

'*Grateful to Life and Death* is a beautiful title.'

'It's the last line of my book—' I was rather surprised to hear her approval as apart from Lyle Blair who changed English Teacher to Grateful to Life and Death, I've not met anyone to approve of the change.

During tea, which was very welcome after the walk, we were joined by—(name not clear at the moment) and his extraordinarily beautiful wife. This man continued the talk on Forest Lawns. It was rather careless of me not to have listened attentively when the visitor's name was mentioned, but I gathered from the talk that was going on that he had come to the States to direct an opera at the New York Metropolitan, that he had directed some outstanding pictures in England, and that he was eminent in the theatre world. I hoped for the best, thinking there would be an occasion for me to catch the sound of his name in due course. When we all rose to go Huxley told him that he could drop me on the way as they were going down the Sunset Boulevard and were in need of someone to show them the way. His wife drove the car, because the gentleman had found the gadget-ridden, left-drive, American car they had rented for the trip as well as the traffic rules, beyond him. They stopped the car in front of my hotel on Sunset Boulevard. I thanked them and said,

'You should come to India and make a picture', 'I would love to; it has always been my ambition to make a picture in India. Can't we discuss it sometime?' 'I'll be in London next month,' I said.

'That will be wonderful. Why don't you give me a call when you are in London?'

'I will take down your number in a minute,' I said, the engine was running as they were in a hurry to reach a party at eight o'clock. I felt awkward to hold them up. But I had to know where I could see him again. He seemed to be a worthwhile man, who knew my books, and also a friend of Graham Greene. I fumbled for my pocket book which I had left behind, while holding a simultaneous conversation with him and his wife. And now suddenly drew up along the driver's window a police-officer on a motor-cycle. He wore a helmet and was grim-looking. He held out his hand and said,

'Your driving license and birthdate,' to the lady.

'Why?'

'You are getting a ticket.'

'What is that?' She asked.

He took out his book and started writing.

'Your birthday? Your name?'

The lady was distraught. She said,

'What has happened?'

'You turned the wrong lane.' The gentleman tried to ask a question or two and said with resignation, 'There is nothing I can do about it. Let her deal with him,' and turned away from the whole thing to me at the other window, and said, 'Please give me something on which I can write my address'. At the other window the policeman was arguing with the lady. He seemed to derive a fiendish delight in tormenting this lovely person.

The lady was saying, 'But I didn't know. . .'

'You should know the rules.'

'What is a wrong lane?'

'You shouldn't have taken it,' the officer said. He handed her a ticket. He was bawling at one window explaining to her the traffic regulations and also what was in store for her at the law court. She was angry and kept telling him that she was a visitor, a new-comer to the country, which only provoked the man to hold out more and more terrifying prospects for her. I felt a tremendous responsibility for the whole situation. If I had not asked them to stop at Highland Motel. . . I apologized aloud, through the window, to the lady on the other side, over the head of the gentleman. She kept asking something of the grim policeman, who wore a steel helmet and looked like a Martian just landed with a ray gun in hand out to disintegrate and atomize the citizens of this earth, and he was bawling something in reply. Her husband had completely detached himself from the whole proceeding. He snatched from my hand a journal I was carrying and wrote on it his name and London telephone number. It was a magazine Huxley had lent me to read a tough article on ESP by someone. I could not still decipher his name. I told him,

'Yes I will telephone, but perhaps you would be busy', wondering by what name to call him on the phone in London.

'Oh, I will be rehearsing. . . you will be welcome.' The lady, 'This is ridiculous, we are returning to New York tomorrow early',

'Well, you will have to go later, that is all,' the police man said.

The motor cycle pattered out. In a quarter of an hour she could start her car again, mastering all its gadgets. They were so preoccupied that I had not the heart to say good-bye to them. On this confused note we parted.

I couldn't make out his name on the magazine cover. I telephoned to Aldous Huxley and learnt that he was none other than Peter Brook, the famous British stage director. Later when I went to London I tried to get in touch with him, but I learnt that he was busy at Stratford-on-Avon conducting the Shakespeare festival. His wife answered the telephone and said, 'Oh, dear, I can't forget that awful evening. Wasn't it dreadful! I will never go to Los Angeles again.'

*

Dr Kaplan picks me up at twelve o'clock and takes me to Columbia pictures to meet the writer-producer Michael Blankfort—fine, sharp, friendly man, who looks like a re-incarnation of Arnold Bennet, with his moustache and chin. Lunch at Naples—a famous Hollywood restaurant and pub, full of atmosphere—low, head-scrapping roof, from which dangle hundreds of wine-baskets in miniature, autographed pictures of a million movie personalities, dim red light, smoke and narrow sofa seats at the tables. I have learnt to manage these luncheons—having my own food (which I call heavy breakfast) earlier in the day and nibbling salad and stuff like that at the parties, the company itself being more important. Kaplan is a brilliant wit, scholar, and conversationalist; and Michael is equal to him. Michael is good enough to inscribe a copy of his novel and give it to me with the remark, 'If I were a painter, I'd have given you a picture, but this is all I can offer'.

Back to hotel, where Dorothy Jones comes to take me to the Twentieth Century Fox. It's easily the biggest studio here. Our public relations takes us first to their chief cameraman, who explains at length their latest lens for use of wide screen and fifty-five millimetre films; and good enough to show us some tests—amazing sweep the lens has without panning, which he demonstrates with sight boards arrayed ahead in a semi-circle— the lens takes it all in one glance; and then close-shot also on the same principal, of any object at a distance of about seven hundred feet. He shows me several charts with enthusiasm.

'Any questions?' he asks.

'Oh, no. It's all so clear I've no questions.' It's difficult for me, in spite of my vague, general interest in technicalities, to maintain an intelligent face while he is talking. He is a man completely submerged in his technicalities, and cannot think for a minute that there could be anything else in life worth thinking or talking about. Moreover, through some initial error somewhere, I have been introduced as a novelist, screen-writer and 'Producer' from India, and it's too late for me to correct the error. It gives me a chance to observe closely technical matters. Next, in the sound department, they explain the changes that the advent of the magnetic tape has brought in. I'm taken through vast, complicated recording rooms.

'You must be familiar with the magnetic—'

'Yes, of course, naturally,' I say. It's all very complex and impressive to me. Sound has always attracted me in a vague way, but I don't understand a thing about it. I manage to essay one intelligent query, suitable for the occasion.

'Are these compatible with fifty-five millimetre frames?' The question, it's a cute one I think, passes the rounds, and they say,

'Well, not exactly yet. . . '

And then we pass on to more theatres. I could probably appreciate it better if I saw something happen there. Mere technicalities bore me; and then our guide takes me to see the 'Lot'—'New York street', 'Ocean and Sky' , ' French village'

'Egypt', 'Blue sea and horizon', 'A London street', all facades used for outdoor scenes, a symbol of 'Maya', as Huxley said, permanently built on several acres of ground. I'm soon out. I catch the bus on Santa Monica. The bus driver is very careless. First he shuts the door with me half-way through, (some day an American is going to be cut longitudinally and only then will they alter the arrangement of doors in their buses) and next he crashes into a new Chevrolet. The cars are stopped. It's extremely calm. No police. Our driver distributes a card round to the bus passengers,

'I'd appreciate, if you gentlemen will fill this,' like a conjuror involving the audience in a trick. I look away. I don't want to be involved in anything. People get very busy writing down.

'Can you pull out your car—?' he suggests to the man whose car has been rammed in.

'Yeah' he says and does so. If it were our country there'd be so much of speech and action and recrimination, and comments from by-standers. Here no one bothers. No argument between the protagonists no accusations or gesticulation They exchange notes and papers—behave like real gentleman in an ancient duel. And then the bus is on its way again; and the car is driven off. Only sign anything is amiss, being a long piece of chromium plated metal which is flung out of the Chevrolet. People are full of praise for the driver of our bus. They have silently, unconsciously become partisans. No one likes the man whose car has been rammed in—not even himself. They mutter,

'It was a terrible piece of driving.'

I feel irritated at having to go out again at eight p.m. I am on the brink of calling off the evening engagement. But Sally won't hear of it. She has fixed it with David so and so the writer. After a hurried meal, I am out again meeting Sally at Hotel Roosevelt. We go by bus to David's home. Find the family quietly settled after dinner—with the daughter at her homework. David is a successful Screen and Television writer, whose speciality is 'Western'. He is not a born writer. He does not like writing; does it only to make money—and hopes to retire, go on a holiday, and take to painting: he has adorned his walls with grotesque, obscure daubs in frame. He may be called the 'Robot' writer. He is evidently very successful and in demand.

Even while we were talking, producers were calling him on the phone. He looks on me, I don't know how. He views other literary work as mere prolific raw material for his screen-version, I suppose. He even mentions that most book writers indulge in a vast quantity of unnecessary writing. However, I'm happy to talk shop with him. His wife evidently has great admiration for the profession and keeps saying that the percentage of human beings that could be called authors is ever so small, while there are doctors, barbers etc., in any number.

*

The Metro-Goldwyn-Mayer visit. The same type of talk with the "International" man. Difficulties with India Government. Bhowani Junction was not shot in India because the Government did not give in writing any agreement that they'd make no demand on its world profits! Strange are the ways of Government and films. Lunch at the famous restaurant, watching the shooting for a while by the famous George Cukor of 'Les Girls', more 'Lot' inspection, New York, French Village, Sea and Forest. While crossing the lawns, a brief shakehand meeting with George Murphy—an old time actor, who says,

'You are from Mysore? I have just met a convent sister from Mysore, who is collecting funds for a high school. She and her companion: they were so charming, like a couple of birds alighting and flying away. I could not help giving a small donation because their appeal is so sincere. . . You know about that school?'

'Name?'

'Christ the King. . .'

'Oh, that is where my daughter studied, it is next door to our house, what's the name of the sister?'

'Bernadine'.

'She was my daughter's teacher.' The world has shrunk suddenly. Who could imagine in these surroundings Bernadine, the kindest of teachers and the most despairing one for my daughter's arithmetic, who often came down to see me and say,'Oh, you must do something about Hema, the poor child needs special attention.' There was nothing I could do about it, arithmetic being as much a terror to me. To hear Bernadine's name again after all these years! Human beings get knit up in all fantastic unbelievable ways, complex and unexpected links like the wiring at the back of a radio panel.

Visit Paramount Studio, which is just a repetition of other studio experiences. My guide the grandson of Zukor, called Adolf Zukor the Second, slow, timid, shy and very intelligent. He keeps saying, 'I don't know what you can see here!' He crashes into a studio where a notice 'Closed' is hung outside; they are shooting a scene with Lizabeth Scott and someone else.

Next engagement, visit to 'Consolidated', a hectic place, where I sit on a bench at the reception, waiting for a man to appear and take me in. There is a spring door in front of me, which is being pulled and pushed continuously—men and women, chatting, preoccupied and in a deadly hurry sweeping in and out. Those who wait at the reception are restless and fidgetty, and those who move do so in a run; never was a spring door more agitated. It is a place where a 16 mm. films are processed and sent off to various television studios, as it seems, exactly with a minute to go for the scheduled programmes. Finally a man turns up and takes me in to show a magnificent colour film on an Indian village made for the Ford Foundation. After the show, offers to drive me in his car to my hotel. An over-active man, who wastes lot of my time by neither letting me go, nor keeping me company, he makes me sit in his car and dashes in and out of various buildings on the way. So that I reach my hotel late in the evening.

A telephone call at my hotel.

'Is that Narayan?'

'Yes, speaking.'

'*Namaste*, Narayanji,' I was surprised.

'Who is speaking please?'

'Kenneth McEldowney.' Another man whom I had lost sight of in Bombay seven years ago. Fantastic contacts really. He had seen my name in *Variety* the trade paper and had tracked me down. Years ago we should have made a picture called Khedda with the background of elephant-trapping in Mysore jungles, he had several reels of it taken in technicolour and wanted me to write a story around the subject. We met in Bombay, discussed plans and then kept writing to each other; a file developed, he

became famous with his picture, directed by Jean Renoir called
The River, but the second picture never came to be done in
spite of a very fat file of letters and cables growing out of it on
my table. Ken McEldowney got into some contractual difficulties with the Government of Mysore, thought it best to abandon
the project altogether, and the loser was myself since I had
already worked on a number of possible stories for him. But it
had an unexpected result. I had gone through so much research
into elephant catching in Mysore forests, where herds live and
flourish and are rounded up through an elaborate system of
drives, that I grew interested in the subject myself, and I may
possibly deserve a doctorate in elephant affairs!. . . This man
telephoned to me today and took me to his home in Bel Air.

'Vedanta Plaza'

In search of Vedanta society of Hollywood on Vine. The
county authorities having cut a Free-way through a corner of
the estates of the Ashram, have compensated by naming the
area officially Vedanta Plaza. Hollywood is full of philosophy
and yoga. At one end of the Sunset Boulevard we have the
Self-Realisation centre with its own chapel, where I spent an
evening listening to a sermon on 'Reincarnation,' where books
by the late Yogananda, and mystic souvenirs, are sold. Young
men and women were listening to the lecture on reincarnation. . . They looked fashionable, modern and young; one
could not think they would be attracted by reincarnation, but
there they were, voluntarily walking in and listening. The
Self-Realization centre incidentally has at its entrance one of
the best vegetarian restaurants in the United States; the first
step in self-realisation is good-food, and that is provided for at
the entrance, after which you could step in to hear a lecture or
buy a book on *vedanta*. At the other terminus of the Sunset
Boulevard four miles away I saw another signboard announcing
Yoga lessons by appointment. Here we have 'Vedanta Plaza'
officially included in the county registers—so that's where
Indian philosophy stands at the present moment in Hollywood,
which seems to me really a versatile place with its technology,
television, aeronautics, world of illusions and the world of

enlightenment. . .

Swami Prabhavananda the head of this Society, is away at Santa Barbara. His next in command is a young person of the name of Swami Vandanananda, who left his family in Mysore when he was seventeen, about twenty years ago, spent over ten years in Almora at the Mission's headquarters in the Himalayas. Like a true sanyasi, as one who has renounced the world, he had not thought of his home or written to any of his relations for over a decade. But talking to me, in that hall—brought back to his mind, Mysore, his home in D. Subbiah Road, his aunt, uncles, and friends, and the Kannada and Tamil in which we spoke induced in him a slight home-sickness, perhaps. I seem to have brought with me a waft of his old life for him. At six o'clock, he left me and went to the chapel to conduct vespers. A number of inmates assembled and sat in silent meditation before a picture of Ramakrishna and the Holy Mother. Lamps were lit, flowers and incense. The prayer went on for a long time; in that stillness, I slipped out, when everyone sat with shut eyes, and wandered in the garden.

Later the swami joined me and took me to the dining hall. There are about 60 American men and women, living in this ashram. They go through a course of studies and ascetic discipline; men and women are necessarily segregated— sometimes they change their minds and return to the mundane world; sometimes a romance develops and they wish to renounce the ascetic life and go out and marry; Swami Prabhavananda, the head of this institution, takes a very generous view of all such second-thoughts and never denies his disciples their freedom of action; some stay in the Ashram for 10 years, become qualified to be called 'Swami', learned, and austere and carrying on the work of this mission in various parts of the world. . .

*

With Aldous Huxley and Gerald Heard to the Los Angeles Medical College, where they address a group of medical men on Mescalin. They dwell on the deepening of consciousness as a means to helping the next phase of evolution which must all be spiritual and mental, men having reached the peak in the material world. Mescalin, Lycergic Acid, are some of the drugs with which Huxley and Heard are experimenting. One memorable sentence of Huxley   in the speech, I forget why he said it, 'Alcohol is incompatible with automobile.' At the end of the meeting my camera goes into action and I manage to take several group photographs with Huxley and Heard. After the meeting, I stop off at Huxley's house, for tea and talk. Later they drive me back downhill at the end of the day as usual. Huxley urges me to come back to the States. I dine at the Self-Realisation Centre Restaurant on the way and go back to my room for packing.

*

Checked out of my room at noon. I had grown rooted to this motel and felt sorry to leave it. The motel lady gave me a room till the evening train-time, free of cost. The whole day messed up by a hope of seeing Gerald Heard, and by the uncertain engagement, with a young man I had met at the Huxley lecture, an under-water specialist. He was threatening to come any minute since seven a.m. to take me out in his car. I had to make Dorothy wait uncertainly at her telephone, although she called nine times to know when she should come for me. Finally the sub-aquatic man turned up at two-thirty in the afternoon, and drove straight to a television studio because he was under the impression that's what I wanted to do. He forgot that he had offered to take me to his house. I wriggled out of this mess; the only wise act for the day on my part being refusal to hand him my roll of exposed negatives, which he wanted to take charge of in order to help me get them developed. Dorothy arrived at 3; and immediately plunged into my travel and packing arrangements. Pack-up and leave motel, seen off by the entire family who manage this motel. The old man said, 'Give my respects to Nehru—he is a sound man.'

GRAND CANYON
AND BEYOND

Grand Canyon

THE word grand had never a grander function to perform. Its mighty quality is a thing that has to be directly felt, and no report at second-hand can ever convey its tremendous impact. It has versatility and modifications in its apparent geological fixity. Yes, now when one comes to think of it the word 'fixity' could never be more misapplied for a thing created by the interaction of water and soil and rock, and mellowed by light and sun. It is a work of art by Nature—a sort of abstraction in which Nature has indulged after having passed through the phases of symmetry and perfect form. Here we have pure abstract forms, colours and chromatic scale from blue to red and grey—so well merged that you would not notice the hundred shades in it. Here are forms which defy classification. They are like South Indian temples, they look like Buddhist temples; we have before us a conglomeration of Mahabalipuram, of Hoysala architecture, various battlements and pyramidal structures, mighty ones, which not the sternest slave-drivers could ever have hoped to erect or copy; chasms, and prototype of every architecture on earth. The resemblance of various formations to temples is so great that they are called 'Shiva temple', 'Brahma temple' and 'Zoroaster temple'. Here all religions meet and merge. It is here you feel with an unbearable agony, a mystic mood; the almighty takes his name here. Here is a performance that overwhelms us with its might.

The sun is setting and I feel it a sacrilege to be writing this instead of keeping my eye on the rocks. It is easy to become incoherent in this presence. I noticed my fellow-passengers in the tour bus uttering involuntary cries at every turn and the word 'temple' was much heard. Those who would not notice a temple anyway involuntarily utter the word. God has shown in the most solid of things—rocks—the highest of elusive abstractions of form. Observing this I get a sympathetic notion of what abstract painters attempt to do. Far down, the Colorado winds its muddy course, and its roar comes out muffled and softened. But the chatter of fellow tourists is rather trying. But it may be remedied, I suppose, by suggesting that silence must be maintained while viewing the chasm.

Before the East lightens, to watch the canyon is to watch an infinite void. At this hour when the sky is still starry—there are seven stars over the void, it looks like the beginning of creation itself. At first there is absolute darkness below, but if you keep looking on, gradually contours and rises become faintly visible—softly emerging to view. At this hour, with only the stars to witness (fortunately they make no noise), absolute silence reigns over the whole scene—everything is absolute here.

Fortunately all the guests in the hotel are asleep. This is one of my own private and special sights of the twilight of the night. Some whisperings rise from the depth, if you will hear it—like the echoes of ocean one hears in the shells. The light of the morning—the first shaft to bring the chasm to view again. I'm waiting for it, but, alas, the bus has already arrived to take me to Williams and end the charm.

Santa Fe

At the Williams station, we learn that the train will be late. No one knows more. There is a casualness about the railways here which I like. A train is heard to approach far away. One man runs out with a flag. The train will pass unless it's flagged. We are all alerted. The man who stops the train for us also does multifarious things—sells tickets, writes on forms, operates the controls, holds out the mail bag, and pushes our luggage into our respective coaches. I don't know if he can be tipped. How can one tip a station master, which perhaps he is? I don't know whether to look on him as a porter or a station superintendent. Finally I take the benefit of the doubt, having tipped so many others.

Leaving Williams the train passes through the deserts of Arizona for hours and hours—huge signposts announcing 'Serpent Gardens', 'Rattle-snake' farms and such attractive places all along the way. The scene is very much like passing from Arsikere to Davangere, dry, sandy, with rusty wrecked cars everywhere.

Lamy at four-fifteen—a small flag-station with the threat of the train pulling out before you are fully out of it. A bus journey and now in Santa Fe actually.

Hotel hunting, and then to La Fonda—single-room without bath for the night; sneaking up the corridor for toilet.

Evening, having no other business, stray into a Cinema. People eat and drink too much inside the hall, constantly going out during the show to fetch noisy things to eat, and of course flirt and woo in their seats, hardly paying any attention to what goes on, on the Vista-Vision, Cinemascope, Perforated, Plastic, Silver-Screen.

At the Mexican restaurant beautiful girls in costume-skirts serving, a lovely music on violin, piano and guitar, slow; soothing tunes (God knows what they are,) restful yellow lights, blue-star-lights and white and red-painted rough wooden furniture—the smiling musicians—all this creates a fit atmos-phere for eating enchilada, beans, and what not. A couple in the other table get up and dance, leaving their dinner for a few minutes and resuming it after the dance. A fat couple whom music has made oblivious, for a moment, of their bulk. Looking at them, I feel like uttering the uncalled-for, uncharitable comment, 'They keep off eating only when they are dancing.'

This morning Mr. Long, Gilpatric's friend, takes charge of me. An ex-official of the State Department. It is a relief to find some one to talk to in this place. It's snowing outside. 'Bring your coat along, and let us go out,' is his first call. He has tracked me at La Fonda, which, I suppose, is a sort of a human lost-property office.

Mr Long drives me to the Museum of Folk Art and explains everything expertly. Introduces me to a number of archaeologists for a couple of minutes at each seat. The Doctorate is back on me. It was only at the Grand Canyon that none called me "Doctor."

Santa Fe has the combined appearance of Monkombu, Krishnarajapuram, Sivaganga and Seringapatam—with its little streets and abodes made of clay and tiles; some of the bigger buildings have about them a touch of the palace of the Nawab of Carnatic at Madras—the same richness of timber and style of construction. Every bit has a romantic interest here—that foot-track might have been an Indian trail, that piece of pottery on the ground an Indian pottery (in fact the great archaeological museum was started by John D. Rockefeller when he came here once and found his children picking up pottery pieces.) Santa Fe flavours constantly of this Indian background—the Indians in deliberate costumes selling souvenirs on the verandha of the Governor's palace. There is a Spanish section in the town—half the persons speak Spanish; the churches and palace of the Governor and the bits of a fortress here and there still have a touch of Spain, the Anglo-American influence since 1846 evidenced by the American post office housed in an unbelievably ancient-looking, quaint mud structure. For a small place too many influences are intermingled here. At the moment the local legislature is in session, and the hotel lobby is full of well-dressed loquacious self-important legislators. Mr Long is busy now lobbying with them for securing a grant of a million dollar for a down-town museum.

'Palmess'

Our guide is an interesting man. He is O.K., but for his frequent fascination for pointing 'Pumice', which he calls 'Palmess', he is somehow fascinated by the rocks. He ought to be a geologist and not a guide.

'It's all "Palmess"—see that—it is red through oxidation, and nothing else, but if you scrap it off it's white. . . see that! that's palmess—'

Seeing that the whole mountain range surrounding us is Lava, 'Palmess', or whatever you call it, he ought to see the absurdity of mentioning it again and again—an average of twice every five minutes. After hours of drive through passes and canyon roads, we arrive at the Bandelier National Monument, where are preserved in a well-ordered museum in that far off place, an amazing collection of relics of Pueblo Indians, who lived in this region about eight centuries ago. Here we have also an outdoor museum of their community village, the Tyuonui ruin, excavated in 1908; and pre-historic dwellings gouged out of the Northern cliff-wall of Frijoles Canyon, one to three stories in height with many cave–rooms in each. This affords me a delicious moment of escape into a dim, pre-historic period, although we are walking in the rain with the elevation making me gasp for breath and feel as if I should bleed at the nose next moment. The guide goes into minute details of the Indian's daily life. I pay little attention to his narration, preferring my own vision of the pre-historic life in this mighty wilderness of Rio Grande Valley, traversed in some places only by trails. But the Finnish girl, who is also on a visit, listens to the guide with interest.

The word 'Indian' constantly gets mixed up. 'I had an Indian visitor' says the guide meaning a visitor like me; and then, 'The Indians were etc.' meaning the navajos or pueblo or the apache. The original confusion caused by Columbus still continues in speech.

On our way back our guide takes us through parts of wonderful scenic beauty, snow-filled trees, and snow covered fields and pines stretching away on both sides. And then he takes us into the nuclear city at Los Alamos, which had been closed to the public for thirteen years. Our guide is thrilled to be passing through it. He points to the cars going ahead. 'Boys returning after their day's work—they never discuss their work even with their wives.' He indulges in an imaginary conversation between a scientist and his wife, as he is about to set forth on a mysterious mission to a testing ground. Our guide is very proud of the fact that Santa Fe was the first to be rocked by a small test atomic explosion. He hints that at Santa Fe, of all places in the country, there is an idea of what's going on in nuclear affairs. His incessant talk suddenly depresses me. A guide should talk less, because his employers are totally at his mercy in a car. It's like having a radio permanently tied to one's ears. His voice rasps and sounds worn out like the voice of some of the over-experienced news-readers of the All India Radio. With all that he is a good man, generous, human, and warm. At the Bandelier site he would not let me approach the ruins in the rain, but insisted on clamping his own hat on my head although he was exposing himself to the cold and revealing an incredible state of baldness.

Forgot to add that we visit an Indian village on our way to Bandelier Monument, in one of the reservations and see some houses and two women, with three children watching them, bake bread. One of the Indian women goes in and brings a loaf of bread wrapped in paper, and hands it to the Finnish girl.

'May I buy It?' she asks taking out her purse.

'No, I'm giving it to you. Please take it,' says the Indian woman in perfect English, much to everybody's astonishment.

This place just looks to me like the back-yard of any home in a Mysore village. And our guide seems to be a familiar figure here.

I have had a full swing of civilization's progress—from the cave-dwellings of pueblo Indian to a fresh, almost wet-paint-smelling nuclear city. Enough history for the day.

Morning get up with travel anxiety stirring in me. Various complications become evident before eleven a.m. It is all more indefinite than a reservation on the Blue Mountain Express at Coimbatore. They want me to buy the ticket but will not confirm a journey. It's all chaotic and without understanding. The air services simply feel that if I don't go fully through, I should claim a refund when I'm back at Santa Fe, and will not understand that I may never re-visit this place. The lady at the 'Indian Detour Section' (it's the travel department of the hotel) is very helpful and works out schemes for me and keeps at the telephone for hours trying to pursuade the airport to see my point of view. All is well that ends well—I get a ticket in the evening, confirmed up to only Memphis!

I have phoned to Monroe Spears to meet me at Nashville tomorrow evening!

Meet Mr Long again and gently resist the various involvements he is planning for me. He tries to take me through the Museum again, but I tell him definitely that I have already seen all of it; he tries to involve me in a lunch, which also I ward off, and then he gives me two tickets for a Eurpides play this evening, saying, generously,

'Take a girl with you for the other ticket.'

'Where is the girl?' I ask.

'The girl who came to our house last night, I forget her name, take her along with you. She is very intelligent.'

When I plead doubt, he says,

'There is another girl—' He takes me across to a shop and introduces me to a chirpy, bright 'girl', a super-active person selling souvenirs, saris from India, and 'Madras' shirts. I wriggle out of this situation too. She informs me incidentally in the few seconds, I am there, that she lost a thirty dollar sari last night. . .

I bid good-bye to Mr Long after all. Call up Mrs R—and spend the evening at her home, while my mind is all bothered about the tickets. She is a sad, forlorn creature, with two children, who keep her fully busy. She is from New York. Coming away here, after living for five years with her parents, and realizing that the children would not grow up satisfactorily under the grand-parent's excessive devotion. She is a fugitive from her parents' home, having fled to the extreme end of the country, thousands of miles away to start life anew, strange driving-force her parents must have exercised. The more pressing question is about Mr R—where is (or was) he? But I shall never know. It's snowing today as I've never seen it before. It's white and brilliant everywhere.

Wayfarer

Visit St Miguel's Church, 'the oldest church' in the United States. In this town one comes across too many 'oldest'. The church has three layer in excavation—of A.D. 1300 revealing Indian bones, of A.D. 1600. Spanish, and over that relics of a later period, which is all left uncovered at the altar. There is a father showing us round and, of course, selling picture postcards and souvenirs. I notice another person, with a simpler camera than mine, trying to photograph the altar. It's his first reel and first clicking! The camera establishes a link between us.

I notice him asking the father about a week-end 'retreat' nearby. We become friends. He is a road-engineer on his way to Los Angeles. An Illinois man going to California to seek his fortune. He arrived but an hour ago in his car, and is passing on to Albuquerque and beyond. I induce him to spend a little more time at Santa Fe. He invites me to go about with him. Find him an extremely noble-minded sensitive young man. We go to Lamy cathedral. In the chapel he kneels and prays. And then he goes up to an adjoining office to enquire about a 'retreat' again. I ask what a 'retreat' means. He explains that there are monastic places where one could spend a week-end in meditation all through. I suggest to him Grand Canyon as a place where one could meditate without any special effort.

He drives me about till one o'clock through Santa Fe and its suburbs, and joins me at lunch in the Mexican restaurant,where the girl has kept ready for me Spanish rice. She calls it pure vegetarian, but God knows what there may be in that red sauce. My companion admires the autographed Hollywood photographs that I have secured for my daughter, which I am carrying around before posting. The waitresses come over to see the photographs and all cry, 'Gee! What a treasure!' (later when I go to a stationer to buy an envelope, the younger assistant cries, 'Gee, you've got real treasure. Be careful with it,' and he takes it in to show to his friends in other departments, and I overhear several 'Gees' coming from there, and the word 'Hema' spelt out aloud—it delights me to hear my daughter's name uttered everywhere!)

After lunch my friend and I part. Well, we may never meet again. We've been together for three hours in all—I feel I have spotted out the finest type of human being. A brief encounter, but a rich, and potent one really.

Harveyism

Harveyism consists in converting rocks, scenery, rivers, canyons, towns and atmosphere, including all their civilizations, into cash-business, by selling them to tourists. Fred Harvey is almost a legendary name here. He has built his hotels right in the style of each place, has a shop selling genuine souvenirs, employs dancers who execute folk dances, starts factories where souvenirs are manufactured, dresses his staff in the costumes of the place and period, and by every effort keeps up the Indian, Mexican, and Spanish qualities of everything from Grand Canyon and Santa Fe to God knows where. I fervently hope that our country may not become so utterly tourized (touristized?) that is turns all its cultural treasures, and antiquities over to Harvey, although there are signs of it—seen in the number of Indian Gods, who have invaded the American homes, and the small slabs of carved temple-chariots that every American tourist brings home with him.

7

GURUKULA IN TENNESSEE

SEWANEE is beautiful with its tall trees and brooks and the houses built in valleys and mountain slopes. Sewanee is a 'Gurukula';—a small college of five hundred boys (no girls admitted), lovely cottages, few and far apart on the hill, tall trees, and in every way a most attractive, little place, where it is possible to practise studies and discipline without any distraction. They do not seem to have even a cinema nearby, nor any of the allurements that grow around the mammoth campuses. The boys by a resolution among themselves are dressed in full suit and tie and look extremely sober (no crew-cut and fancy jersey here); the staff are all quiet and intelligent and devoted. I am a guest in the home of Professor Monroe Spears. Monroe's home is a scholar's retreat, set amidst dogwood in bloom, filled with books, music, and pictures, with no television or radio in the house, and run by the generous, ever-cheerful Betty; her daughter little Julie, the moment she saw me, promptly announced, 'I love you. I'll marry you,' but cancelled it in a huff three days later when I left, because she was not being taken along.

*

Up early in order to be ready for a class of boys in Monroe's college. At nine we march into his class. Monroe writes on the black board 'Assignment—R.K. Narayan'. He reads to the class Graham Greene's introductions to two of my books. The normal work of the class has been suspended. I speak to the boys on my books, the problems of a writer and answer their questions. Afternoon Monroe drives me around and shows me the sights of Sewanee, beautiful valley-views from various points of vantage, and a drive to an immense cross standing on a hillock a memorial to the Youth killed in the war of 1914-18. Evening a large party in Monroe's house. I hold a glass of sherry as a courtesy—but a sip of it sends my head reeling and I put it away. I meet here the entire society of Sewanee, and quite a number of them say how much they appreciate Tagore's writings. Nowhere else have I come across so many who mention Tagore. A lady has come wearing ivory pendants and ear-drops made in India in my honour, and feels happy when I assure her they are genuine. Betty, our hostess, has dressed herself in Indian material. This is an Indian day at Sewanee. The crowd leaves as fast as it gathers. After dinner a number of college boys arrive; and we sit in a semi-circle. I answer questions; even such a one as 'Has the sacred cow been abolished in India?'

'Why do you want it to be abolished?'

'Food is scarce in India, we learn, would it not be better economy for people to eat beef?'

'Cow is also scarce in India, and it's better they are not eaten off but allowed to provide the much-needed milk as long as they can, and when they go dry we like to leave them free to live an honourable, retired life instead of killing them—just as you treat old-age pensioners who may not be active now, but who are none the less treated considerately.'

*

After lunch, to Monteagle to catch a bus for Nashville where I shall take the plane for Washington D.C. The bus depot is displaying in its waiting hall 'For Coloured' and 'For Whites' notices. Even in the bus the white passengers are the first to take their seats. The conductor manoeuvres in such a manner that the coloured men can get in only after the whites are seated. The convention seems to be that the last seat should be occupied by coloured passengers. White passengers blink unhappily when I get in. Each tries to cover a vacant seat next to him with an overcoat or hat for fear that I may attempt to occupy a prohibited seat and create a 'situation'. I pass on straight to where two negroes are sitting, and they make place for me. There are still four seats vacant in our row, but none comes there. A fat white man and his short wife get into the bus on the way, but prefer to stand on their feet for seventy miles rather than sit down next to me. The short wife cannot reach the strap on the roof of the bus, and the fat husband cannot keep on his feet; they suffer hell, yet they prefer to stand and travel rather than sit by my side. At the Nashville bus terminal I see 'Coloured' and 'White' notices everywhere, and immediately take a taxi for the air-port, and 'check' my luggage, have coffee, and correct the novel for two hours, in an effort to forget the problems of human complexion.

8

WASHINGTON D.C. AND ONWARD

Bus and tram drive through the capital, which is definitely a Government town, with Government buildings, Government quarters, Government offices, and my only human contacts are all with the officials of Indian embassy. I cannot move around too much owing to the very cold wind freezing my ears. I wrap the muffler over my head, like a Ooty bus driver and create a sight for everyone to gaze at! Visit Washington Memorial, Jefferson Memorial and Lincoln Memorial. This is a city of mighty monuments. This whole city is one of offices, office buildings, protocol, and office-talk. It has the stamp of New Delhi and Bangalore combined in it.

Washington is the cleanest city I've seen. Its one other attraction is the sweetness of its taxi service. Anywhere to anywhere however circuitous or delayed it might be, it is just 40 cents or 60 cents according to zone, and no tips mind you. I've found the most enchanting taxi-service on earth.

*

'I've been a barber longer than your years—I've been a barber for fifty years—starting at fifteen. I'm now sixty-five. I was in England in the first world war. I've educated three sons. I've four grand-children. I've always managed to work and keep myself going. Work is my religion—you come from India? Great country—but never have been there. You are a lucky fellow to have travelled so much . . . you want your hair clipped close? I can take out anything, but never put back even one—remember that when you ask me to cut. Crew-cut! Horrible! Hopeless! I'll never never give any one a crew-cut. I've cut hair for fifty years; I know my job. Why don't you leave that to me?. . . well good-bye, it's nice seeing you. If you are happy I am pleased. Those who come here must always go back happy, that's what I like.'—Hotel barber. All the time he was cutting, he had a cigar in his mouth. I gave him a 5-dollar note, not being certain what would be the correct payment. He took a dollar and a half and returned the balance.

★

On the train to New York. Ideal time to try and read the manuscript of my novel, which I wrote in Berkeley. I try to read it, not as an author, but as a novel-reader who has picked it up for a train journey. Difficult to keep up the pretence—the book being in my long-hand manuscript; still I manage. Well-settled in my parlour seat, I start with the first line of my novel beginning 'Raju welcomed the intrusion', and try to feel curious about further developments. I notice through a corner of my eye the passing piers, jetty, cranes, hangars, and the sky line of steel works, aluminium or plastic manufacturing concerns, and oily shores and tumble-down houses, noting the heavy industrial stamp on this land-scape, still I am quite absorbed in *The Guide,* and realise with a great deal of relief for the first time that it does not bore. The journey takes about four hours and gives one an ideal situation for reading for the first time one's novel.

I can only specify this part as the east coast, was it Hudson or what river, there was one of those huge American rivers looking like the ocean or was it the Atlantic itself? I couldn't say. Everything in this country looks like an ocean. The so called lakes of Chicago are like the Bay of Bengal! I am no good at geographical details and I am not interested in industry, and so I can only say I passed a number of chimneys and coast line and ships in harbour and so forth. What a contrast to other parts of the country,—the Californian open spaces and hills, the mountainous green portions of Mid-West with their mighty trees and suggestion of tremendous sweep, the desert region of

Arizona, and the slick governmental touch of Washington, and the versatility of New York. This is a thoroughly industrial area and the one which is perhaps responsible for keeping America in prosperity and modernity. But I have not the time to brood on this scene too long, for one thing it doesn't interest me, for another I find Raju's career more inviting. We pass Philadelphia and I recollect with a sigh how many lapses I may be charged with for not answering the numerous letters from Norman Brown of Pennsylvania University, asking me to address the India Society group. He also suggested in his letter that they were starting Marathi and Gujarati studies and that my valuable opinion on those courses would be welcome. I had to write to say that they could sooner ask me to suggest a course of studies in Swahili and Yiddish and that I knew only Tamil and Kannada, and none other of the fourteen Indian languages. To which their only answer was to repeat their invitation. I put away the letter not knowing what I should do about it. Now the brief halt at Philadelphia pricks my conscience. After seeing the Asia group in Berkeley I fight shy of such organizations anywhere. I sit back with my novel. Raju is making passes at the archaeologist's wife...

9

NEW YORK

CALL Keith Jennison (of the Viking Press) first thing in the day. He invites me to lunch. When I go there, he apologizes for having made a mistake, as he has already another lunch engagement. He is happy and relieved to know that the book is finished. He, with one or two others, listens to my narration of my novel. He likes the story, and feels very hopeful for the book. My manuscript being what it is, I have to revert to the ancient system of oral story-telling. I think a story acquires an extra dimension in this kind of narration and it's such a labour-saving device. I think an ideal situation would be where one gets a royalty for dictating at a publisher's office.

*

Snatch a snack at a restaurant. On an impulse phone to Faubion, who tells me to jump into a cab and go there at once. 'Some persons who adore you are here, you must see them.' So I'm there soon, find a lot of people assembled in his house. The Bowers are absolutely overwhelming. After an hour we go to a party—where we meet Anna Magnani, the Director of Metropolitan Museum Art, a psychiatrist, an Italian publisher's representative, fiction editor of the *New Yorker*, and so on. We are soon in the thick of introductions. Santha and Faubion are so generous in referring to me that everyone views me with awe. It's Anna Magnani's birthday, and there is a chorus of happy-birthday-to-you and raising of glasses.

*

Major part of the day taken up in shifting to a room on the eleventh floor—looking over Madison Avenue and the river of traffic there. All day in the room—letters, Kitchen-arrangement, and, in general, putting one's house in order. Lyle Blair turned up in the flesh. Wonderful to meet him after so many years of friendly correspondence. At first sight I know it should be Lyle and none else.

Went down to see him off and then post a letter. At the Post Office in thirty-fourth street, gave the packet for weighing. Looking at the address, the counter clerk, 'India?—Oh, how is India now?'

'Very well, thank you.'

'Things O.K. now?'

'Perfect.'

'Fifty-cents—Oh!. . .'

'Can I put more in?'

'Sure, just a little over half ounce—write more, put plenty more; do write to all your aunts, uncles, and companions, and tell them how do you do, it'll still cost only fifty cents. Photographs? Wonderful go ahead. . . well how are things at home? I mean in India. All O.K.? How are the new conditions?' 'Wonderful. They are doing big things in a big way there; tremendous projects, industrial schemes and so forth.'

'Oh, Isn't that marvellous! Now do they make shirts and suits and machinery and things like that?'

'Yes, yes, that's just what they are doing.'

'What's that coat you are wearing? Is that imported?' 'No, made in India.'

'Really! what wonderful stuff! You mean to say they make such things there?'

'Yes, all this wool comes from Kashmir. . .' I say casually, not quite convinced within myself, and dreading lest he should go off at a tangent and start an investigation of the Kashmir issue.

Lyle Blair

Meet Lyle Blair at Bleeker Street, off Washington Square, at an address he has given. It is drizzling but I manage to find the place and press the bell. A girl comes down the stairs and leads me to a room on the second floor (third according to American step-counting system), where there is another girl. Lyle is expected. They know my name and I see my books on their shelves; they work in a publishing firm and they are Lyle's friends. He comes in presently. He settles in a sofa and I see him at his best—arguing, contradicting, emphasizing, and overwhelming all through whether the question be publishing, Kashmir, or anything. He has a lot of resemblance to an aggressive uncle of mine, especially when he goes into breath-taking philosophical turns. We repair to an Italian restaurant for dinner. I get an enormous plate of egg-plant fried in cheese and can eat only half of it. During the dinner Lyle declares: 'I'm terrified for your future, because you are going to be eaten up by the lions of New York; but let me tell you, in future you may do well or ill, but to have written *The English Teacher* is enough achievement for a life time. You won't do it again and can't even if you attempt.'

'Why are you so arrogant that you'll not let people do what they like for you? It pleases them to do something for you; please give them that liberty,' he says later.

'No, but I'd like to be able to do something in return. . .'

'You write. You've given them *The English Teacher* and that's enough. They like to do something in return for it. Let them do it.' And so, I had to watch his friend go down two flights and into the rain to fetch me ice cream,—for which I'd expressed a preference inadvertantly at the restaurant.

Our talks and discussions go on until midnight. Lyle constantly swears at a cat, which is a guest here, really belonging to someone involved in a motor accident and now in hospital, the cat alone escaping unhurt; and a parakeet which goes on pecking at its own image in a mirror creating an uproar, the cage kept out of reach of the cat on a shelf high up. Lyle calls the parakeet 'Narcissus'. The cat like all New York cats, is fat and bloated. It can't go out; it goes to the window and keeps looking out through the glass, at the drunken and the Bohemian population of the street below; Lyle who is somehow averse to the parakeet hopes that the cat will go up and make a meal of it, but it is perfectly safe here. The cat is so indolent and demoralized by synthetic cat-food, that she can't spring up to the cage on the ledge. When the cat needs exercise, they give her cat's-nip to stir her into action— a small bundle of it flung on the floor makes the cat execute a variety of dance and capering. Who discovered this? The same civilization which provides tinned-food for the cat and saves it the bother of hunting mice and bird, also provides it the cat's-nip for exercise—a rather comprehensive civilization. It's happening to the cat what's happened to human being since his days of cave-dwelling and food hunting.

Get up at ten, and do not leave the room till five in the evening. Hear the drums of the St Patricks Day parade on the Fifth Avenue, but cannot go down because I feel too lazy to dress. Glimpse of a uniformed procession with band on Madison Avenue from my window—regret that I cannot photograph it although there is such a beautiful sunlight outside. I keep revising my book before lunch and after lunch—but have not progressed beyond five pages for the whole day. Every word on examination looks doubtful.

At five o'clock, take a subway on Lexington, change to a local somewhere and go up to Bleeker Street, which is full of tottering drunkards today, due to St Patricks festivities. After my San Francisco experience I've a fear of being held up. Go up to Lyle's friend's house, where a fine dinner is prepared for all of us. Lyle has a terrific cold today, but is still in form.

After dinner I asked, 'When do you plan to visit India?'* 'I have been there once, years ago,' he says. This is rather a surprise for me. Lyle has a tendency to unfold surprises. I ask for details. 'I knew something of the country through my uncle.'

'Who was your uncle?' I ask.

'Robert Flaherty, you know the man who directed The Elephant Boy, who brought Sabu to the States, etc., etc.' It is unnecessary to dwell on Flaherty's achievements at this distance, but the sequel to a mention of him is interesting. I say, 'Do you know that he shot the Elephant Boy in Mysore where I live, where there are elephant-jungles all around?' And then I

---

*Since writing this Lyle has visited me in Mysore.

add 'And I know his daughter who has settled in Mysore. I have met her a few times, and we did a feature together for a radio programme on the trapping of elephants. She was our narrator.' This stings Lyle into unexpected action. 'Do you mean to say that you have known Barbara?' Wait a minute. I want you to talk to her mother.

'Where is she?'

'At Vermont, five hundred miles away. You must tell her about Barbara.' I try to excuse myself. 'Well no time for it, let us think of it later, I don't know the lady. . .' He brushes aside all my objections, and pulls me along to the other room where there is the telephone. He dials the operator and cries,

'I want Vermont, Mrs Frances Flaherty.'

'Number?'

'I don't know the number. Don't insist on it.' He adopts a sudden, bullying tone and says,

'I don't know the number but I must talk to the lady immediately I am giving you her name and address, you will have to find her number somehow. . .' And he puts down the receiver and waits till the operator calls him again and I hear him shout,

'You have the number? Fine, why do you tell me what it is? I am not interested. Give me the connection.' He turns to me and says, 'We will get the connection now. It is twelve years since we saw Barbara off. You must tell her mother about her.'

'Tell her what?' I ask anxiously. He ignores my question. He gets the connection to Vermont. It is eleven-thirty in the night and it is evident that the population of Vermont has retired long ago. They are pulled out of their beds, and feel naturally anxious at being called at that hour. After a few minutes Lyle speaks into the telephone.

'I have a friend here from India who has known Barbara. He is from Mysore.' He hands me the telephone.

It is Mrs Flaherty. She is thrilled to hear about her daughter; she asks numerous questions about her, how she looks now, what radio programme we did together, and what I thought of her voice. She is overwhelmed, as she says, 'How I wish I were going with you to India to see Barbara!' Lyle feels gratified, 'You have made one soul supremely happy.'

*

Evening went out on a ramble. Never realized till now that I was living so close to the famous Empire State Building, though I was seeing its tower everyday for over a week. This is the worst of over-working on a novel—you become blind to the tallest building in the world. Proximity makes us indifferent, although, in Laxmipuram I'd have been eloquent about it or hearing about it. Must go up some time, but I can't bring myself to the point of joining the regular sight-seers anywhere, though it ought to be the most sensible, and practical thing to do. But who cares to be sensible and practical? I may probably go back home without ever ascending the Empire State Building but then I shall have done nothing worse than any confirmed citizen of New York. I watch for a while people buy tickets and move up to the elevator,wondering where they came from. Glance through all the tremendous 'promotion' material around. One would have thought a building like the Empire State was in no need of promotion (my little nephew at home can say exactly how high it is). But there it is. Its statistics are impressive, but I could not accept their own list of eight wonders of the world (which they display at the window—in which the Empire State finds a place but not the Taj Mahal.)

Food for the Gods

Lyle Blair's party for me at Algonquin to celebrate the publication of the American edition of my *Mr Sampath*. Algonquin party room is so exclusive that only fifty guests are invited. Everyone is there, the Indian Consul General, the Australian Ambassador and his wife, the Breits, the Bowers, Gilpatric, a girl from *Look* looking like Ingrid Bergman, two priests, two publishers of paper-backs, the President of Michigan University and the Vice-President, Professor Blackman, the Viking Press, Balaraman, many men and women from the writing world, whose names I never catch, and above all the Indian delegate at the United Nations Organisation, who sits in a chair and says to me when introduced, 'I am dictating my third novel to my secretary, having completed my second in eight weeks. I am surprised where all the idea comes from. In the midst of all my office work, I am able to do it. I'd like to talk to you—what is your address?' I mention my hotel and its whereabouts, which does not interest him. He says, cutting me short, 'Why don't you call up my secretary and leave your telephone number with her so that I may get in touch with you sometime.' I leave him at that.

After the party a small, compact group stay on for supper. Two New York paper-back publishers, whom we shall indicate as Mr A and Mr B, a priest, a girl in a red gown, Lyle, and myself. We have a corner to ourselves at the dining hall of Algonquin. Publisher A sitting opposite to me, leans across to say,

'I like your *Financial Expert*. It is your best book.'

'I like your *Bachelor of Arts* better; it's my favourite,' says publisher B sitting to my right.

'William Faulkner, Hemingway, and Narayan are the world's three great living writers', says A.

I blush to record this, but do it for documentary purposes. After the discussions have continued on these lines for a while, I feel I ought to assert my modesty— I interrupt them to say, 'Thank you, but not yet. . .' But my own view and judgment are of the least consequence and no one pays any attention to it. They brush me aside and repeat, 'Hemingway, Faulkner and Narayan, the three greatest living. . .'

'Take out Hemingway and put in Graham Greene. Faulkner, Narayan, and Graham Greene,' says Lyle.

'I don't like Graham Greene,' says one.

'Why not?' asks the priest in a kindly tone.

'His obsession with catholic theology upsets me.'

'What is wrong in it?'

'I don't like it, that is all'.

'Come, come, you can't dismiss it so easily. You have to explain what upsets you in Catholic theology.'

From this mild beginning a veritable storm soon developed. The waiters came and went. Each whispered his or her choice in their ears. They brought the food and placed it around. The napkins were spread on laps; shining cutlery was picked up, but they were hardly put to their legitimate use; they were being flourished to add punch to argument. Plates remained untouched. One or the other would draw the plate into position and carve a bit, but before he could stick the fork in there would occur a theological exasperation and up would go the knife and fork to emphasize a point or to meet the challenge. Lyle who had ordered a joint done brown, could not proceed beyond pecking at it once every ten minutes. The lady in red was the only one who proceeded smoothly with her dinner, and then of course myself. Out of courtesy I waited for a while to be joined by others, but I found my asparagus soup growing cold. The waiters were bringing in the courses mechanically. I quietly followed the example of the lady in red and ate my food unobtrusively. I quietly worked my way through, and had arrived at the stage of baked apple and cream, but found the rest still at the stage of Torment, taking a morsel to the lip and withdrawing it swiftly to rebut an affront. What really stirred, them to such a pitch was a thing that I never really understood. It was all too obscure, too much in the realm of higher theology, the minutiae of belief. The only thing that I caught was that publisher A was out to puncture the priest. Mr A was saying, 'Answer my question first. Could a betrayer be an enemy?'

'He has to be a friend. How can an enemy betray?' A sinister laughter followed. When it subsided Mr A said, with a quiet firmness, 'I am a much better priest than you are. Take off that dog collar you are wearing, what is that for?'

'John! John!' pleaded the priest, 'Don't .lose yourself so utterly. Pull yourself together.'

'I am all right. I can look after myself quite well. It is you who needs pulling together. You are no better than the drunken, dissolute priests one encounters in Graham Greene's novels.' The priest could do nothing more than cry, 'John! John!' in a tone of tremendous appeal, and then he pointed at me and said, 'We have a distinguished guest with us tonight. Let us not insult him by our unseemly acts.' Which seemed to have the desired effect as Mr A bowed deeply to me from his seat and said, 'I apologize to you sir for any inconvenience caused.' The greater inconvenience was to be the centre of attention now, and so I said, 'Not at all, not at all. Don't mind me. Go on with your discussions. Please don't stop them on my account,' which was accepted with gusto and publisher B turned to the priest and said,

'You have not really answered John's question.'

'Why should I? Am I bound to answer?' A fresh sinister guffaw followed this. The two publishers seemed pleased at the effect they had produced; they leaned over to each other and spoke under their breath and laughed among themselves. Lyle thought that the time had come for him to assert himself. He held his arms over his head and said, 'All are my guests here; I won't have anyone insulted at this table. Let us have this discussion some other time. Let us eat now.' This was really a sound, practical suggestion. The time was nearly eleven. Three hours had passed since the food had been served. I had noticed through a corner of my eye the progress of the night at the restaurant. All the other guests had left. The linen had been taken off all the tables. Lights were put out, half the hall was in darkness; on the outer fringe a couple of waiters stood patiently. Cordiality was restored, plates were passed round. One heard not theological remarks but, 'Did you order this chicken?' 'Oh, dear, I must abandon this soup. . . Fish! Lovely!' Everybody settled down cheerfully to eat, drew their chairs closer, rolled up their sleeves, with the exception of the lady in red and myself who were lingering over the desserts in order to let the rest catch up with us. It would have gone on well, but for the arrival of a steward at this moment and a whispered message to Lyle who had just tasted his joint. Lyle immediately cried, 'Listen friends, here is the steward come to say that Mr. . . the manager of the hotel, wants us to accept a round of drinks in honour of this evening. . . Please give him our thanks. Surely. Won't he join us?'

'He had to go away, sir, but he requested that you should accept his hospitality, Champagne, sir?' 'Yes, why not? There are', he counted heads, six here. 'Give him our thanks, won't you?' Conviviality was restored, but the food receded once again into the background. One or two got up to visit the wash. I was relieved to find that religion had gone to the background. When they resumed their seats, they were all smiling. 'We must really get on with the dinner,' Lyle said.

'Of course, of course,' everyone agreed.

The time was nearly eleven-thirty. I noticed less rancour

now, the priest as well as the rest were laughing while arguing. I
felt relieved. The priest turned to the lady in red and said,
'While all of us are talking you are silent, why don't you say
something?' She merely replied between drinks, 'I have nothing
to say.' She was the one person who had pursued with a steady
aim her food and drink, and now she seemed a little bored.
'What can she say?' said Mr A pugnaciously. 'You are a priest,
and it is up to you to talk and save our souls. Here I am asking,
what are you a priest for, if you can't answer a simple question?'
The priest merely looked at him, pointed at me and said, 'Let us
not make fools of ourselves before him. Let us talk it over
tomorrow.' 'There he is,' he said pointing at me. 'He is an
Indian, he is from the East. He knows these problems inside
out. It must all look childish to him. Let us close up now. He is
watching us silently. Remember he is dead sober, while we are
drunk. Let us end all this talk,' at this Mr B leaned to say to me,
'you see sir, we are a young nation, we don't know the answer,
we long to have an answer to our questions.' He held his hand
to his heart as if there were excruciating pangs there. 'We are a
tortured nation, that is why we seek an answer. It is no problem
for you really, because you know the answer to all the
questions.' I had to say, 'No, I don't think I know the answers, I
haven't even understood the questions, you know.' He just
brushed aside my protestations, 'No you know the answers. I
know you know because your *Financial Expert* contains in it
answers to all our questions.'

'Does it?' I asked rather surprised. 'Where?'

'The last portions of the book,' he said.

'I didn't know,' I said completely baffled.

'You wouldn't know, but we know. We can read them,' he
said, and it left me marvelling at the theological implications of
my fiction. He came close to me and said, 'But you must
sympathize with us, we are all the time struggling and
searching. You must watch us closely. You don't have to do
anything except put down all this conversation as you have
heard it, and that will be a wonderful conversation piece. I
know you can do it because I admire your *Financial Expert*' (I
have acted on his advice and hence this narrative.)

He pointed to Mr A with a good deal of sympathy, 'His

eagerness to know is very real, his enquiry is honest.'

'I must have an answer,' Mr A said, stung by this reminder. He looked straight ahead at the priest and cried, 'I insist upon your answering my question.'

'John, John, you are starting it all over again.'

'Tell him something, why do you spurn his question?' said his friend.

'We have no business to be arrogant, it is arrogance which is at the bottom of all our troubles,' began Lyle. He is ever fond of the word 'arrogance' and brings it up anywhere.

'The priest is the one who is arrogant,' Mr A cried with passion. 'What is he wearing that dog collar for, let him pull it out and throw it away.' Saying this he proceeded to attack his dinner.

At this, the priest looked at him fixedly and said, 'You have provoked me enough. I'll answer your question after you answer mine. Tell me who you are, what you are, and where you come from?' This question stung Mr A unexpectedly. He was livid with rage.

(Later, I understood that Mr A came from a part of the country which was supposed to be known for its display of bigotry.)

'It has nothing to do with my problem.'

'Gentleman let us eat our food,' Lyle said. The priest repeated, 'John, who are you? What are you? Where do you come from?' In answer to it Mr A pushed his chair back and his plates away. 'I refuse to sit at the same table with this. . .priest. You are a. . . priest. No better than a Graham Greene character. I will say it again and again.' He turned to me and said extending his hand, 'I apologize for going, but I can't sit at this table. It has been nice meeting you. Good bye.' He walked away.

Jackie

My handwriting generally reduces typists to a state of apathy and defeatism. After years of writing I have not yet evolved a clear system of writing. I am often asked how I write, whether I type or write long-hand— I do both. Whether typed or written, while revising I generally write between lines; sometimes there may be twenty lines of original writing, to a page, but twenty five between-line writing, and further corrections on all the white spaces around a page. Most of this disfiguring of a page is unconsciously done, the main aim being to get through the work and put it in shape.

I had now an occasion to study my own methods dispassionately when I tried to find someone to type the manuscript of my new novel *The Guide*. No doubt sitting in the train from Washington, I could get through the manuscript but I did not stop to think how it might strike anyone else trying to read the manuscript. I realized my folly only when I promised to deliver the manuscript to Viking on a certain date, looked for someone to type my manuscript. Through various recommendations, I got a number of persons willing to take up the job, but at one look at a page and they would invariably say, 'At the moment, we are busy—' I was in despair. After trying everywhere, one afternoon, after lunch, I appealed to Faubion to help me. He said, 'I'll ask Jackie to type your work.' He took the telephone, spoke, and said to me, 'Jackie will meet you at your hotel at eleven o'clock tomorrow morning. She will do your work,' he said confidently.

I asked, 'She may look at my manuscript and go away as others have done.'

'She won't,' Faubion said, 'I know her.'

Next day she was in my room punctually at eleven. She went through ten pages of my manuscript and said, 'This is nothing compared to what Mr Bowers gave me when I had to type his book on The Theatre. I will make a start tonight and give you about thirty pages a day. I will leave blank spaces for doubtful words.' She came back with thirty pages next day, but before proceeding with further work she noted on a slip of paper words which confounded her. It tied me to a routine again. Every evening I broke away from a late party with the excuse, 'I have to have thirty pages ready by morning for Jackie.'

Jackie has found an added interest in the novel because the book was written in Berkeley where she studied, and she is from Oakland nearby. What made her settle in New York? After graduation from Berkeley College, she had an ambition to join the stage, and so came to New York. While attempting to work her way on to Broadway, she has to maintain herself by freelance typing work. The frustrations in this country operate mostly in the world of arts and letters, and not in the ordinary walks of life as in our country. I have cheered her up by saying that some day at Broadway I should visit a theatre, see her starred, tell everyone that she typed my novel once, and go back-stage to greet her.

★

'Your women don't look worn out at all—they always look so soft and slow—while here all the time one has to be catching a sub-way or a bus, working, working. Indian women don't work? They do! But probably not much to do—sharing the house-work with six other wives. I heard that an Indian husband had seven wives—all living under the same roof: one to make the bed, another to wash dishes, a third to take care of the linen, fourth to run the vacuum cleaner, and another to take the waste basket and garbage and so on; it must be a great relief—' says Myrtle who comes every morning to tidy up my room.

★

Jackie explains how she is enjoying typing my novel; finds Raju's character engrossing; confesses that last night she nearly resolved to give me up, because she could not make out certain passages however much she tried. I believe she must have cried a little. But finally victory was hers, and she has managed her quota, with but three errors. I assure her that she has got through the worst patch (which I very much doubt) in my manuscript. I decide not to bother her to work at the weekend because she is planning to go to New Jersey, where she has her boy-friend. 'He is a Chemist, you know, but really calm without any neurosis, a wonderful man. He is thirty. I know I can be happy with him. He is devoted to music and the theatre and we have common interests.'

'Why don't you marry him? What are you waiting for?'

'Ah, can't decide that fast. It will take time. We are not able to make up our minds yet, about a great many things. . .'

'But don't you love each other? If you do, it should blindly sweep aside all other considerations, you know.' She merely repeats, 'Can't decide that fast.'

G.G.

Walk down Lexington Avenue, to John Gunther's house. He opens the door with the warmest greeting, and takes me inside. His wife Jane introduces me to a lady sitting on a sofa, wearing a gray gown. While we are talking Faubion, Santha, and Donald, burst in. After settling down, Faubion says to me, 'Tell us about your mystic experiences.' I say something evasive, but he will not let me go. I plead for time, but he says, 'Now, I want to hear, I must hear all about your mystic experience. . .' The lady in grey says something very profound and subtle. I am impressed with her talk. And then, it's time for all of us to go. I suddenly remember that I must know Balaraman's address where I'm dining this evening. I take out the telephone book on Gunther's table and fumble with it. Anthony West arrives. Santha and Faubion go out and wait for me on the road. The lady in gray moves out, and before going she comes up to me, nods a farewell, presses my arm. When I join them on the road Faubion asks,
'Can you guess who that lady is!'
'No.'
'Try.'
'No, I don't know,' I say. 'Only thing I can guess about her is that she must be continental, perhaps an artist—'. 'She is Greta Garbo,' says Faubion.

We are all going to be late for our various engagements. Faubion hails a cab and bundles all of us in. Santha says, 'I'm getting worried about you. I don't know how you are going to reach Balaraman's house at West End Avenue. As our taxi turns on Third Avenue, we see Garbo standing on the kerb, waiting for a cab. After they get off at their place, I take the taxi on and reach Balaraman's house only an hour late, but Balaraman is used to my ways and has forbearance.

*

After a couple of hours of work in the morning, lunch with Anthony West and Donald Keene at Chateau-briand. Anthony is leaving tomorrow for Japan and India. I have promised to meet him in India. Donald gives him a number of Japanese addresses. After lunch we walk down Lexington, visit a book shop, a picture gallery and finally on with Anthony to the end of 80th street. We plan to meet in Mysore (actually Anthony arrived ahead and was waiting for me at Bombay). At the sub-way, telephone to Santha, and she asks me to go to their house at once. I find them celebrating Ruth's birthday (Ruth has been with them for years and helps them with housework). Numerous guests drop in. My good friend from India, Dr Narayan Menon phones from somewhere that he's just arrived and will be dropping in soon. Santha says that Garbo wishes to meet me again. She called this morning to say that she wants to meet 'that man from India' again. It's a rare instance of her wanting to see anyone. She's only four friends in the world; John and Jane Gunther, Santha and Faubion.

We move to a party in someone's house. Many men and women whose names I don't catch; and a Spanish novelist, who writes in English, and who has many complaints against publishers in general. An artist from *New Yorker* button-holes me, 'I'm looking for any system of teaching which has abolished duality.' I mention Shankara and others, but he will not accept anyone, proves everytime that a man who attacks duality is dual himself, and so forth! I waste a little time arguing with him. Faubion is ensnared in this discussion and cries out, 'Oh, Narayan, help me with an argument.' Narayan Menon arrives, but before one can say 'Hallo' to him, he is cornered by this 'Duality' man.

*

Ill with an attack of allergy. All day have to remain indoors. It is snowing heavily outside. All day scratching and coughing, awful life, but still keep up progress with the novel; Jackie comes and goes as usual. Evening telephone Gil and cancel an engagement at Oberlin. The thought of travel aggravates my allergy. Gil suggests a Doctor. Call him on the phone. Engagement at one-thirty p.m. next day.

Rain and sleet outside. Cab to 70th street. Doctor takes me to bits. Examines me like a mechanic looking over a derelict automobile. Stripped to the waist, I move from room to room. Scréens my chest. Pricks my finger-tip for blood. He is worried about an infection at the base of my lung. But assures there is nothing to worry about. Gives me pills and an injection. He is a normal, healthy doctor, with normal aversions and suspicions about abnormal conditions. He orders grimly, 'Go back to your room and stay in bed.'

Afternoon with Gil. His wife and children are away in Washington and he is in sole charge of the house. He manages quite well, able to pick a meal at a restaurant or fix something for himself. That is not his main worry but the white mouse, which his daughter has left in his charge with strict injunction to keep it alive till she comes back. It is kept in a small cage in the bathroom and Gil gets quite anxious about its welfare, often running in to see and assure himself that it is flourishing. 'Only four days more; I hope nothing will happen to it before then. Bah! what a responsibility!'

The afternoon is fine and sunny. We go out, we pass through Frick's Museum, enchanted by Rembrandt's self-portrait and the collection of Dutch paintings. People are moving east and west and along the kerb. We walk in the Central Park and enjoy the sight of children at play, and finally we come to a spot where groups of men are playing chequers on park tables; it is a characteristic of New York; chequer-players in parks, on a bright day there will always be a set of players concentrating on their game and a circle of on-looker equally absorbed in the same game. After this round of orthodox sight-seeing, we walk back to Gil's house. He toasts a couple of muffins for me in his kitchen, and makes sandwiches and tea. We sit at the dinner table for over an hour with these. It is most peaceful and enjoyable. We wonder what to do next, and come to the conclusion that the best engagement would be to lounge in his study and talk. We go through this engagement so thoroughly that it is past nine-thirty when we look at the time again. We must have got quite drunk on a few glasses of orange juice and a great deal of conversation. Gil is one of those great souls who can give and take in conversation and his interests are wide-ranging, let us say, from Mysore to Santa Fe, touching all the worthwhile personalities and politics therein. I suspect that he does not let television invade his home mainly for fear that it might destroy the art of conversation.

*

It is almost a routine with me now. I keep working away on my novel till three in the afternoon and telephone to Narayan Menon at Prince George's to know if he is free. He always says, 'Most welcome, come immediately.' It is a fresh joy everyday to meet Narayan Menon, who elaborately bows and opens the door and asks 'What can I give you, Sir?' as if we were formal strangers, and then he always gives me news of what he did since we last met—a composer he lunched with or a recording of his music, or news from home; and there is always his Veena, lying on a cushion, covered with a brightly patterned, hand-woven cloth. It brings the whole air of India into this room in Prince George. It is a tempting instrument. Menon plays for a moment and generally hands it over to me, and a few tunes in *Bhairavi* and *Kambodhi* and we appreciate each other unreservedly, and start out at about five, hail a cab and get down at Faubion's house at E Sixty-third street; where we invariably find a large and lively gathering of all kinds of personalities from the theatre, publishing and literary world.

G.G.

Adopting all the precautions suggested by Faubion, I am ready to meet Garbo again at lunch in Santha's house. Garbo never likes to be reminded of films or of her past association with them.

Garbo and her best friend in the world Jane Gunther arrive. Ruth has made for me Macaroni and cheese, cucumber sandwich, and fruits. It is fascinating to pretend that I am not aware of the personality of Garbo but that I take her to be a common-place woman of New York. Films and Television and all kinds of shows are so much a part and parcel of our lives that one inadvertently stumbles into these forbidden topics and retreats hastily. 'When I was in Hollywood. . .' I begin and then a look from Jane or Faubion and I suddenly withdraw from the topic, and cover it up with something less dangerous, as Faubion threatens that if anyone so much as mentions film-life, Garbo is likely to get up, open the door, and go out unceremoniously. It is a very trying situation. I think this is a unique instance, of someone passionately craving for obscurity and oblivion, while plagued all the time by fame and immortality. For this reason we had to leave out Narayan Menon, who was very eager to join us today. He even said, 'I will stay quietly in a corner and never say a word. All that I want is just a glimpse of Garbo. My memory of her is as Queen Christina, and Ninotchka and Anna Karenina; please allow me a glimpse of her.' But unfortunately he had to be told, 'Another time, please,' for it is generally observed that G.G. (as she is addressed) just shuts up, or turns back and retreats if she finds a stranger in the company.

The lunch is a success. The talk is all about religion, mysticism, evolution, and reincarnation. G.G. asks, 'Why have we been created, why have we been made to suffer, undergo pain, and then, what is the meaning of all this? Why? Why?' Her voice as she says it is rich and modulated as if she were speaking the lines in a play. I have to find an answer because evidently she has enough faith in me to think I can give her an answer. I can only view her problem from the point of view of *Karma* and the evolution of a being from birth to birth. She argues about it. The practice of meditation could probably give an answer in a flash. She confesses, 'I don't know how to meditate. What do you meditate upon?' I am generally reluctant to speak about my inner convictions, but there is no way of avoiding it now. Her enquiry is so earnest that I cannot help speaking to her about it. I have to confess to her that we are taught the *Gayatri mantra*. She wants me to repeat it and explain its meaning. She follows my words with the greatest attention; I explain to her the power of the syllable according to *Mantra Shastra*, the meditative principle, the picture of the Goddess on which the mind has to dwell; the symbolism of the image, and so forth. After listening to me, she says,

'It is all too advanced for me. You belong to a nation which is highly advanced in these matters. When and how can we reach your level of thinking and understanding?'

'Sooner or later,' is all that I could reply.

'May not be in a single birth, but after a series of them, that is why we believe in a sequence of births,' I say attempting to sound as prosaic as possible and avoiding at all costs the tone of pontificality.

Time to disperse. She rises asking me, 'Do you owe those teeth of yours to your vegetarian diet? Do all Indian have strong teeth?'

'Even the poorest have strong and resplendent teeth in our country.'

Before leaving she brings her palms together in an Indian salute.

'Where did you learn it?' I ask.

'Many years ago at Hollywood, I used to visit the Vedanta Society, and the discourses and lessons there gave me so much peace. . .' she passed on, probably disturbed at the word 'Hollywood' that had slipped from her own lips. A little later I left. While crossing the first Avenue I saw her and Jane ahead. They waved before disappearing from view.

*

Rather crowded since the moment I got up at nine o'clock. I had only an hour to spare for myself. The rest of the day till midnight handed over to others. Till one in the afternoon revised the last ten pages of my manuscript and Jackie came in exactly at one to take them away. A big burden is off my back. To think that tomorrow I shall have no manuscript to revise! Delicious thought. After disposing of Jackie, took a cab and rushed to the Indian Consul's home for lunch; being Tamil New Year's day, this good Consul has remembered to ask me in for a South Indian meal. Back to the hotel and then on to Narayan Menon's room to play the Veena. After dinner off to Faubion's for a night party, where Narayan Menon is to play the Veena, explaining South Indian music to the guests.

Really a gorgeous gathering of music and theatre: Leopold Stokowski, John Gunther, Martha Graham, Edward G. Robinson, all distinguished men and women. Menon plays Veena. Ed G. Robinson is a marvellous personality. When he lights his cigar, you couldn t think he was not on the stage. He has a pleasing gruffness and drawl in his voice, and listens to you with puckered brow and a slight tilt of his head. He asks about India, wants to visit it someday. As usual I generously extend him an invitation. About his pictures he says, 'I felt so rich when I had my picture collection around me. They meant something to me. Now I feel really poor. . . They had to be sold owing to a stupid Californian law of divorce. Some Greek fellow has bought them. I've only fourteen left. But I'll collect again. I can't help it—but those that are gone are gone.' He lightly thumps his heart to show the pain—his voice, expression, and gestures are memorable and sad. He invites me to see his Middle of the Night. 'I have seen it, I think you've the problem of the middle aged man beautifully brought out in it.'

'There is no middle age,' he declares. 'We are middle aged when we are born, or have no middle age at all. Life is important . . . You write about the common denominator in all humanity—all nations and men are one. Your books, I am sure, will bring out the idea. Perhaps, when I travel on I shall be able to understand the same message, and carry it back with me to this country. I am not interested in curiosities, but in common denominators. I hope, when I come to India, you will help me understand the Indian mind.'

Pleasures of Indecision

Earlier in the evening helped Menon to get his air ticket for Washington. He likes to remain undecided and confessed, 'Once I've bought the ticket, I'm always racked with the feeling that I've done the wrong thing, and want to cancel the journey.' I can understand this temperament more easily than anyone else can. I decide to write a short piece on the 'Pleasures and perils of indecision in New York'.

New York is one place in the world where you cannot afford to be indecisive, whether it be the business of crossing the road at the right moment or booking one's passage for a future journey. But such decisiveness has not yet come into my nature. I like to leave the door open for a retreat at anytime. And so it is with trepidation that I visit the fifty-fourth floor of the

Rockefeller Foundation. The fifty-fifth is a place where the visitors are allowed to indulge in semi-dreamy talk, because it is the floor of the directors who generally put up with the vagaries of their grantees who are drawn from all over the world and are of a varied kind. For instance if Gil is not actually pressed for time, he is generally very tolerant and understanding of all the contradictory plans and proposals I keep making; but it won't work on the fifty-fourth floor, which I have always named the zone of stern realities. Here we have the controller to whom you have to give very concrete replies if you have to draw the funds allotted to you. The *per diem* and the travel grant and the non-taxable portion and clearance from income-tax, and so on and so forth are all very concrete and very important. The most vigilant actions are performed here. And then the travel section on the same floor, where they just ask on what day you propose to leave and where you want to go and when and what you propose to do until you reach your home in Mysore three months later. It is extremely unrealistic for me to think so far ahead. The travel officer makes the reservations all along the way, warning me, 'Better have some reservation on hand than none . . . you may alter these things later as you go along . . . You will arrive in Zurich at ten a.m. and leave . . .' With his pencil poised over a tablet he awaits my decision, an acutely uncomfortable situation for me. There is no such thing as making a casual statement and then building up on it little by little, knocking down a bit here smoothing out something else there and so on. The pleasures of indecision are not permitted here. You have to think fast, precisely. And then the other room where your baggage is handled. You are directed there to an officer who can parcel anything and pack it off to the ends of the earth. Whether it is a large shipping case or the little test tube containing a serum or a mosquito (often required by the medical section of the Foundation), he is the man to do it. His greatest triumph was in the case of a professor from Mysore who had lost all his baggage, did not know where, between India and the United States. He did not have even a blade for his morning shave when he arrived in New York. He confessed his trouble to the officer, who contacted the air ports all over the route, spoke long distance to everyone on earth, traced, and within a week the professor got all his baggage back, placed in a Pullman in which he was travelling to Boston.

'I have some baggage to be sent to Mysore,' I begin.

'How many? How many pieces?'

'May be four,' I say.

Paper and pencil are poised ready for action now. I am rather terrified; 'I have not packed anything and I don't know.'

So I say, 'May be one or two more.'

'Shall we say six packages?'

'Yes.' He at once telephones to someone, 'Six packages to be picked up at nine in the morning tomorrow at hotel . . .' He turns to me and says, 'The truck will call at nine. Will you advise the desk clerk at your hotel?' I feel amazed at the speed of these decisions, and would like to postpone the whole thing, 'I have not packed them properly yet,' I begin.

'Oh, it doesn't matter at all. You just lock the boxes and put all the other stuff into a cardboard case . . . I will give you some twine and labels and tabs. You just tie up roughly everything and stick the labels with your address and we will do the rest. Don't bother to pack, we will do all that. We will put them in bigger cases, waterproof and seal them, so that you will receive them all intact at your end. Leave it to us. O.K.?' This speed does not suit me. I begin, 'I have just come to find out about these things from you. It will be quite a while before I leave, the date is not settled yet. As soon as I am able to know the date, I will see you again.' He says, 'Any time you are ready, you just give us twenty-four hours notice.'

'Yes, yes,' I say in a business-like manner, 'Thanks a lot,' and I leave the fifty-fourth floor with the greatest relief at having put off so many decisions. The practical men on this floor may perhaps be wondering how I ever got through any place at any time at all. I am as much surprised indeed, but as I write, I am back at home after visiting most of the countries I planned to visit and all my baggage has arrived intact.

March of Dime

Having nothing definite to do I decide to walk without aim as I often do in Mysore. Up Fifth Avenue to 63rd street, watching shop-windows, crowds and the flux of New York, and back to my hotel through Madison Avenue. At Vanderbilt Square a man says, 'Hot chestnut sir, very good.' I have always been curious to handle and taste chestnut which I have only read about. He takes them from over a brazier and gives me a packet. 'Twenty-five cents, sir.' A handful, for the same money you could buy a first-rate dinner in our country. I try to taste it, cracking its shell and eating it in a public highway, wondering how it may strike the New York citizens, but they are a generous lot, who do not mind an active chestnut-muncher walking in their midst. A young man in a heavy coat, a few yards behind, stops every passer-by and says something. I want to know what he is saying to everyone, and slow down till he comes up alongside. I stare at him with so much interest that he sidles up to me,

'Can you spare a dime?'

'Why?' I ask.

'I need it,' he says. He would rather walk slowly while talking than stand in one place. I realize that he does not like to be noticed. I adjust my pace. He looks quite respectable; his shoes are sound, his coat is good, his hat was quite sightly. Quite a presentable young man.

'What do you do with a dime?'

'What does one do with money? Buy myself food, I suppose, that is all.'

'You look young and strong. Don't you do any work to earn?'

'Sure, off and on. I do some work. I was a truck assistant and got off the job only two weeks ago because I was sick and in New York Hospital. I am just coming out of the hospital.'

'Can't you find another job?'

'Yeah, sure I could.' But, he lowers his voice further, 'I am the sort that can't stick in one place long. Rolling-stone sort, you know.'

'Why can't you stick in one place?'

'Well, that's how I am', he says philosophically.

'How do you manage then?'

'Like this.' I understand that in other words he is a born vagrant who was pleased to be so—rather a rare specimen in a place like New York. I gladly part with a dime for the pleasure of seeing this rare specimen in New York, and he goes off. Before leaving I tell him, 'If you hate to work and would prefer to risk living on charities in the streets, you should be in our country, where such a life is understood better.'

Loose Coin

One of the minor skirmishes that I was engaged in daily with Menon, was in the matter of tips. He was of a liberal disposition but I always felt that he was over-doing it. He seemed to set aside ten dollars a day for tips alone. It was of course his own business but I felt that he was responsible for creating a bearish tendency in the tip market, and was also creating a social order consisting of good-tippers and mean-tippers, in which (latter) category I feared that I would be thrown . . . Not that I don't want to give a legitimate tip where it may be due, but this man's habit of scattering coins somehow oppressed me. Everyday I protested against it. He tipped even where it was not expected and he surprised many a tip-receiver by suddenly darting at him a quarter dollar. He believed in tipping not less than a quarter each time and multiples of quarter—fifty cents for a cab ride costing thirty, one dollar for lunch and so on; twenty-five for one who flicked the dust off his coat and said, 'How do you do, sir?', twenty-five to one who said at the door 'Another nicer day h'm'. My impression was that since the moment of leaving his room (no, even before leaving his room, he parted with cash when his breakfast tray was removed), going down the elevator, crossing the lobby, and passing through the door he handed coins to whoever looked at him. He asked a hall porter, 'What time does the train for Washington leave?' (which, in any case, he was not taking), and when he brought a reply, he handed him a quarter. He handed a quarter to the elevator boy when he said, 'Nice day sir?' or 'How are you this morning?', and of course the doorman who whistled for a taxi got his share; not to mention the usual quarter dollar for care-takers of his coat in various buildings. He paid enormous tips all through lunch and dinner, and I need not explain what he did with his cash when he travelled in a train: the porter got three times his legitimate charge of twenty-five cents per bags, and of course every time the train attendant peeped in to ask, 'Did you want anything, sir?' he got his dues. This was absurd. I felt that my friend was carrying it too far. It induced in one a peculiar view of the American currency. If Menon's practice was carried to its logical limit, none of the loose coins one got in the country, was ever meant for one's personal use; all of them were for giving away. The coinage seemed to be so devised that you could not keep it. Starting with the smallest coin, let us say the one cent piece. It is just there to help you to know your weight. At every street corner, drug store, and sub-way there are automatic machines to show you your weight, for tuppence you may have your weight and fate indicated simultaneously (as they say 'Wate and Fate'), the five-cent piece is for automatic machines once again, you can get chewing gum of any sort for a five-cent coin, Kleenex tissues, or anything in that line, the next coin the dime, ten-cent has a specialized and restricted function as it is useless for tips (I heard an old cab-driver reminiscencing, refer to a millionaire of half a century ago, who took a cab-ride everyday to his office, as 'that bastard was a dime-tipper.') But the dime has its functions. It is used mostly for the wayside telephone talks. Any other coin that is put in obstructs operations and will not stay in. (In quite a number of instances, I have discovered a quarter dollar slip out the moment the receiver was lifted, left there no doubt by some hasty dime-less phone talker). Not knowing what to do with it I have often asked the operator what to do with it and she would say, 'Put it back please, thank you,' which I did, but I was not sure if it stayed there long. The dime is also useful for provoking Juke-box music in cafes. The quarter dollar has its functions; it is the basic tip for cab, train service, shoe-shine, and of course the basic fee for the red-cap railway porter, and if you don't have to go shamefaced you must add a quarter to it. After all, these coins seem to belong to the public and have an impersonal touch about them, and Menon seemed to be right in disposing of them at that speed.

Whether a tip has earned the complete approval of the recipient or not may be judged by the taxi driver's saying before leaving. 'Watch your step, sir,' instead of just pulling up the meter flag and starting off. So also the elevator boy when he says 'Watch your step,' you may be sure you will be expected to remember him when you leave. He does nòt expect an everyday tip, he is more practical minded. You are under his constant scrutiny, you can never go away without his knowledge (you may venture to use the steps occasionally but not again and again if you live on the fourteenth floor), and he expects you to settle his account when you leave. My friend Menon, we may judge his popularity by this, was the one person who was repeatedly told wherever he turned, 'Watch your step, sir.'

The big fifty-cent piece, is the most coveted and admired coin among tip-collectors. But it combines in it, unlike the lesser coins, both personal and impersonal utility—that is you may pass it occasionally to pay off a charge and also say, 'Keep the change.'

The dollar bill is the only currency which is meant completely for your personal use, which means that you may keep it until you are obliged to change it into its components once it is split into components, you lose your hold on it; it becomes again something for Menon to distribute. It is a fact that everyone is aware of, as one may easily judge from the fact that even the surliest bus driver gives change for a dollar without a minute's hesitation, nowhere else in the world do you get so much co-operation for changing a higher currency into a lower one. In our own country every bus displays prominently the notice; 'Please tender exact fare, don't ask for change.' In the United States you have only to hold out a bill and the driver's fingers travel automatically to a number of little cylinders on the dash-board, and draw out dime, quarter and fifty, as if they were drawing milk from the teats of a cow.

After visiting Paris and Rome I came to the conclusion that New York has the most equitable system of tip-collecting. The morning coffee and a small roll costs 300 francs plus forty-five in tips in any Paris hotel, and then there is a final addition of fifteen per cent to the total bill when you leave, for what are called 'service charges'. You are generally told that you don't have to pay further tips beyond this, but someone or the other keeps greeting you significantly in your hotel, like the elevator-boy in a Rome hotel who kept asking whenever I was closetted with him, 'Well sir, I am going off-duty at eleven tomorrow;

what time are you leaving? I would like to say goodbye to you.' I found a number of others too wanting to say goodbye to me, and I asked the manager whether I was expected to pay further tips beyond what had been collected in the bill. He said, 'Not at all necessary, sir, but there are some guests who like to give; and in that case we don't interfere, sir.' This meant tips twice over—once in the bill and again without the bill. 'Oh, it does take such a long time for all that to be divided and come to us,' wailed my bellhop, when we discuss the subject.

In London the system is gradually coming, but they are very gentle about it and the scales are also very modest. About six-pence for a short run delights the London cabman, and a shilling for longer runs. When I displayed forgetfulness once, the cabman said, 'This is the exact fare sir! Perhaps you wanted to add six pence, sir?' Gentle beings.

In our own country tips are not inevitable, and the technique of collection is neither systematic nor standardized, although an extra eight annas now and then will certainly earn the undying gratitude of any railway porter or a barber. I wonder if Menon, after his return home, finds his pockets unbearably heavy with loose coin.

'Finis'

As it always happens while completing the revisions on a manuscript I think I worked from morning ten to evening ten continuously,—Jackie walking in for an hour or two morning, afternoon, and evening, to put in the corrections on all the four copies. Painful, boring job, but there is nothing one can do about it. At ten-thirty on a Thursday night, we finish all work on the manuscript. What a joy! I see Jackie off at the sub-way at the Fourth Avenue and return home to sleep. Friday, delivery of the manuscript to Keith Jennison as promised. We celebrate it with a lunch. Later Faubion insists upon opening a bottle of champagne, when I meet him at his house to announce the handing of the manuscript to Vikings.

*

Ravi Shankar's *Sitar* recital at the annexe of the Museum of

Modern Art, before a distinguished gathering of musicians, composers, music critics, and above all lovers of music. On Ravi's request Narayan Menon and myself leave our chairs and sit down on the carpet, Indian fashion. Many others follow this example, and sit on the carpet although it is difficult for anyone to sit down in a suit with shoes on, but they put themselves through this trial as a tribute to the music from India. Ravi explains to the gathering that in India the convention is to express openly appreciation of a recital all through its course, and that the proximity of the listener and his reactions, such as little cries of delight and even the nodding of head, are vital to an inspired performance, and that he misses it in this country where the convention is for listeners to sit still, maintaining a sort of grim silence throughout . . .

Ravi has brought incense sticks from India and has lit them in a corner, and has spread an Indian carpet on the dais, and has dressed himself and his accompanists in *dhoti* and *jibba*. Against this background providing the colour and fragrance of India, he plays pure classical music which transports the audience—establishing the truth of the matter that the highest form of music transcends boundaries and classification. The atmosphere of India is further authenticated by a large cockroach which peeps from under the platform. . .

Passing down a street in Greenwich village suddenly come upon Circle-in-the-Square Theatre, and peeping down its doorway I see Jackie sitting at a table, unrecognizable in a resplendent evening gown. I was always used to seeing her in her working clothes. She has reason to dress herself festively today. She tells me in between answering telephone calls and selling tickets for Eugene O'Neill's *Iceman Cometh* that she is engaged to Jerry, who came down from New Jersey in the afternoon and proposed at lunch. As we are talking, all sorts of people are passing in and out, and she has to answer a dozen enquiries every minute. I leave her for a while and go out for coffee, come upon a book-shop where I see a copy of Santha's book offered at half-a-dollar. I take it, the bookseller regretting that he did not demand a bigger price when he learns that I know the author and intend to get autograph on it.

I go back to Circle-in-the-Square and instantly recognize

Jerry as he waits for Jackie to come out. They celebrate their engagement at a restaurant with me as the sole guest. After that a walk through the Washington Square observing the loungers, and chequer-players on the park bench. They drop me at Helen Hays theatre where Faubion has got me tickets to see Eugene O' Neill's *Long Day's Journey into the Night*—story of a southern family disintegrating through dope, drink, niggardliness and sloth, continuing to disintegrate, and doing nothing about it. I seem to get nothing but disintegration to watch whenever I go to a theatre, beginning with Macbeth which I saw some time ago. Thanks to Paul Sherbert I saw *Orpheus Descending* a couple of days later. Again it concerns personalities who have gone to pieces.

*

With Menon to old Greenwich by train in response to Ann Laughlin's invitation to visit her home. An hour's journey and we are in Connecticut country, a retreat lasting a whole afternoon, from the bustle of New York into an ancient home set in a vast ground, surrounded with apple trees in bloom, brooks, and the greenest of lawns, with the enchantment occasionally broken by the flight of jet planes overhead.

*

Menon takes me to a Chinese restaurant to meet Cartier-Bresson and his wife. Cartier-Bresson wants to see the work of an Indian photographer, and explains his philosophy thus, 'The camera is a limited instrument. It is the photographer who makes it a living medium. He should watch his subject, and take it. Composition is a sense of geometry actually; the quality of life and its expression must be caught accurately. Facial expressions are things like clouds which float by. They change from moment to moment and are gone before you know it. You can never say, smile again, please, it can never be done. Human expression is fluid, ever-changing, evanescent. For instance, your expression as you say, "Is that so?" can never be repeated, or be the same again. I don't know how to say it. But I'm looking for a photographer, who doesn't imitate the West, but has an Indian quality. He must watch, run round, and catch big events in an original way. Twenty photographers. will be clicking the subject, but it's not that, that I have in mind. The photograph must show where he (the photographer) is, what he does and how he searches for the right, original situation.'

G.G.

Lunch at Santha's—other guests: Greta Garbo and Jane. Garbo was delighted when I accepted a cigarette from her; and called aloud everyone to watch my performance. She showed me her diary of engagements to prove how little she was wanted. She peeped into my pocket-books and exclaimed 'Ah, telephone numbers and addresses everywhere!' She was lively and talkative. She took out her own diary to show me the entries, 'I have a bad hand forgive me. I'm ashamed to show it, but see these—so many blanks; and these names are my doctors—the one who operated my foot, my dentist and the other is a beauty parlour man. Nobody is interested. Nobody calls; you see how blank my pocket-book is!'

'If only you wanted—' I said.

She said she was going to South of France for a vacation; where her only activity day in and day out would be to pick up pebbles in the garden, collect them in an old bucket and fling them over the wall. And then she recounted her early story of how a young man was very devoted to her at one time. But she always wore an out-size men's sweater, and never bothered about her appearance. It came near a marriage proposal. But the young man's mother said to Garbo, 'Won't you dress prettily like other girls of your age? How well you would look if you took the trouble!' G.G. was so hurt by the implication of this remark that she walked out of their house and never saw the young man again.

After lunch we part, G.G. saying, 'How I wish we could stop time from moving and always taking us on to a moment of parting! Good-bye.'

MORE ABOUT PENGUINS

For further information about books available from Penguins in India write to Penguin Books (India) Ltd, B4/246, Safdarjung Enclave, New Delhi 110 029.

In the UK: For a complete list of books available from Penguins in the United Kingdom write to Dept. EP, Penguin Books Ltd, Harmondsworth, Middlesex UB7 0DA.

In the U.S.A.: For a complete list of books available from Penguins in the United States write to Dept. DG, Penguin Books, 299 Murray Hill Parkway, East Rutherford, New Jersey 07073.

In Canada: For a complete list of books available from Penguins in Canada write to Penguin Books Canada Ltd, 2801 John Street, Markham, Ontario L3R 1B4.

In Australia: For a complete list of books available from Penguins in Australia write to the Marketing Department, Penguin Books Australia Ltd, P.O. Box 257, Ringwood, Victoria 3134.

In New Zealand: For a complete list of books available from Penguins in New Zealand write to the Marketing Department, Penguin Books (N.Z.) Ltd, Private Bag, Takapuna, Auckland 9.

A WRITER'S NIGHTMARE
R.K. Narayan

R.K. Narayan, perhaps India's best-known living writer, is better known as a novelist but his essays are as delightful and enchanting as his stories and novels. *A Writer's Nightmare* includes essays on subjects as diverse as weddings, higher mathematics, South Indian coffee, umbrellas, monkeys, the caste system—all sorts of topics, simple and not so simple, which reveal the very essence of India.

'(A book) to be dipped into and savoured'—*Sunday*

A DEATH IN DELHI :
Modern Hindi Short Stories
Translated & Edited by
Gordon C. Roadarmel

A collection of brilliant new stories from the
writers who have revolutionized Hindi literature over the past forty years. The short
stories in this volume take up from where
Premchand (the greatest writer Hindi has
ever produced) and his immediate succes-
sors left off and offer the reader an excellent
and entertaining introduction to the diversi-
ty and richness that the modern short story
at its best can offer. Among the writers
represented are Nirmal Verma, Krishna
Baldev Vaid, Shekhar Joshi Phanishwar-
nath 'Renu', Gyanranjan and Mohan
Rakesh.

'By far the best collection of recent Hindi
short stories to have appeared in English'.
—*David Rubin*

GOLDEN GIRL

P.T. Usha
with Lokesh Sharma

The enthralling story of a sickly village girl who rose to become India's greatest athlete. In this candid and engaging autobiography, P.T. Usha talks, in great detail of her meteoric career that began in a tiny village on the Kerala coast in 1964—the drudgery, the heartbreak, the pain, the joy of winning—and ended in a blaze of glory at the Asian Games in Seoul where she won four gold medals and one silver.

'Rich in content'—*The Times of India*